I0818092

ENSNARED

TABLE OF CONTENTS

The Road Not Taken

Two roads diverged in a yellow wood,
And sorry I could not travel both
And be one traveler, long I stood
And looked down one as far as I could
To where it bent in the undergrowth;

Then took the other, as just as fair
And having perhaps the better claim,
Because it was grassy and wanted wear;
Though as for that, the passing there
Had worn them really about the same,

And both that morning equally lay
In leaves no step had trodden black
Oh, I kept the first for another day!
Yet knowing how way leads on to way,
I doubted if I should ever come back.

I shall be telling this with a sigh
Somewhere ages and ages hence:
Two roads diverged in a wood, and I,
I took the one less traveled by,
And that has made all the difference.

~ Robert Lee Frost

PROLOGUE

The one thing Marianne held onto steadfast as she was falling from the sky was her rosary. Clenched to her heart, she held onto it for dear life in the hope that the messiah himself would appear before her and catch her falling body as he had caught her heart. The dreams persisted for many nights, and even months. On the mattress she would lay, blood-drenched and dying, and clutching at her breast. She had spoken the words "Father forgive me" many times with outstretched arms searching for hope. He would kiss and gently levitate her as though within her bodice there contained the seeds of life from which he could resurrect himself.

Every morning she awoke drained of energy; her essence stolen from her; believing her fate to be an inevitable one. Condemned to suffer as she had suffered, she felt she was paying dearly for crimes committed in a past life. A concubine of God, she awoke every morning married and sullied no different than the day before. Her wedding vows renewed, she had only to recite the incantations to summon her messiah. Isolated and cold with no one to care for but herself, she had only to fear the presence of her savior in the cold dark. The violation of her body was never welcomed although she did nothing to prevent him from planting his seed inside her. With each passing night, the veil separating her savior's realm from her own had thinned. This rescuer became far less illusory not only in her mind but in her body as well. She never thought to ask herself why she had such dreams or even to question her sanity. She simply allowed herself to be subjected to retribution. She would have greatly welcomed an explanation for such bizarre and recurring events, but she was taught never to ask questions.

The morning rain was welcomed in her confines. She appeared less distant than the day before. Her dress was made of fine Indian silk, but it had been tattered by her hands when she had suddenly burst into a maddening rage that poisoned even the air she breathed. Her nose was aquiline, and her eyes were green. When she became enraged, her eyes would become as blue as the ocean's wavering tides. Reagan entered her chambers and looked at her longingly, wanting the old Marianne back.

"Have you had those dreams again," asked Reagan, "are you still pondering what they mean?" Marianne merely gleamed at him and fell back onto her bed.

"When do I never have those dreams," replied Marianne. "They come to me every night and every morning I hope to break free from them."

"Perhaps," replied Reagan, "you need to see a hypnotherapist. This has been going on for far too long and I am worried for you."

Marianne lazily lifted herself off of the bed and proceeded to walk across the room as though in a daze. "I know you think me unwell Reagan. I know you grow weary of my tribulations, but I believe I must see these dreams through until I come to an answer in my own time; of my own free will."

Reagan filled with concern looked at Marianne and holding her tightly in his arms said: "as you wish but I think it best you rid yourself of these obtrusions. They are not only burdening you, but they are consuming me as well." Marianne began to undress and slipped into denim pants and a plain white dress shirt. She tossed her hair back into a ponytail and left Reagan staring drearily into her eyes and without saying a word patted him on his back.

Marianne left her bedchamber and headed for the living room. She took out her laptop and began to research the significance of falling in dreams. She was never one to believe in therapy because in one's subconscious lay all the answers to one's past and present demise. With images of angels, demons, and warlocks, flitting about on her screen, she soon grew tired of her research. She would resume in a few hours. She left her laptop and went out into the backyard to take her mind off things. She thought if I walk for a bit, my mind will soon calm itself and I would forget the haunting images that have permanently etched my mind.

ONE

DAYDREAM DELUSIONS

It was May 6, 2019, and Marianne and her friends were running amok on the fairgrounds in southeast Essex. There were fireworks in the air, and people hollering about on roller coaster rides. The four of them, alive and serene, were happy to have finally graduated from both the hard knocks of life and the University of East London. It was a time to celebrate. A milestone in their lives just passed and a new chapter was about to begin; friendship forged forever in the heat of the summer. Marcus, Joan, and Ewan were all too happy to join Marianne in what would be the best summer of their lives. They were gleefully standing in line for the Leviathan ride which would see the lot of them more than 300 feet in the air, dropping virtually at 90 degrees to their pleasant delight. Whilst waiting their turn, Marianne notices a lone man standing alongside the edge of a haunted house. He appeared weary yet solemn. He had straight dark eyebrows, distanced a good deal from his face giving him an open, inviting appearance. His hair was dark, soft and shoulder-length. His nose, though curved, suited his face very well. He seemed isolated; carrying an invisible weight inside his soul just waiting for that moment when someone would ease his strain. Marianne continued to glance furtively at him. He was unusually thin, gaunt, and pale. He was both monstrous and beautiful at the same time. She was instantly fascinated. Then, suddenly, the man looks at Marianne as though the entire time he could feel her gaze. Marianne, without hesitation, looked away while her heart raced. She could see her friends had moved up in the queue and raced forward to catch up with them. Thinking the man had left his post, Marianne looks back only to see his gaze never left hers. He appeared livid. Marianne tried to calm herself and look away, but she could not. His face was stern this time and somewhat menacing. Marianne thought "shit, I'm in trouble now". The man walked towards her, and Marianne frightfully looked in front of her to see if people had moved forward in line and then looked behind her only to see that more people had joined the queue. She could not move forward or backwards, and the man was fast approaching. Fearing the worst, Marianne began to breathe heavily. She wanted to scream for help, but she muffled her face with her hands until a group of partygoers had walked past her and without warning, the man had disappeared – as though into thin air! She was certain he was heading towards her and then like nothing at all, he dematerialized. Marianne thought she was going crazy. She knew she had seen him. Her friends called out to her to come forward and take their seats on the ride and without a care in the world, Marianne was happy to join them.

Reagan was walking the fairgrounds and watching the passersby. He liked it when people smiled at him. He felt less alone. He was intrigued that people were intrigued by him though most would shudder at his zombie-like appearance and scurry away. His mind raced with vivid thoughts of the woman who held his gaze. It wasn't a fatal attraction but rather he sensed a pain in her that fed his inner demon. She had numbed herself to her pain, but he could feel it miles away. That pain was intoxicating to him. What was she hiding underneath her scarlet scars? He was hungry and she was his next meal, having fasted for several weeks. This woman carried the weight of her world in her heart. She had gone through things young ones often shouldn't go through, but she never wavered. She held onto hope and let the pain slide through her fingers like the grains of sand of a cool summer's beach. He read her mind and he could see her aged 7 being bullied by schoolmates, aged 15 sexually assaulted by an ex-lover, aged 21 mugged and left for dead in a back alley. She was estranged from her father and her mother passed away when she was 12. She did not live a life of glamour, but she survived and made the most of it. She could fly into a sudden rage if she felt it was necessary, but she kept to herself and kept her demons at bay with methamphetamine and music. He wanted to tell her she was more than the sum of her trauma. Beyond her glazed eyes, lay a spirit so bright that even a demon such as he would shudder in fear. He enjoyed the scent of her. He enjoyed seeing the many facets of her being, one completely opposite the other, encased in her slender frame. He would normally grab such a frail creature and tear it limb from limb; ending its life knowing it deserved such a fate. No one would even glimpse its disappearance. But she was different. She had an overwhelming sense of urgency to let her light shine. It was as though nothing could diminish her inner light and the harder something tried to diminish it, the more it would beam brighter. He hardly encountered such a creature. She is the first in centuries to have stirred him in such a powerful way. He decided he would follow her and her friends to these fairgrounds and watch her silently like he always does of his victims.

TWO

STRANGE HAPPENSTANCE

As my friends and I left the amusement park, I headed west, by car, with Ewan to my apartment. I was exhausted and grateful for the ride home. Ewan was gracious enough to eat with me, at Subway, before leaving me at my front door. I was happy to spend one last night with him before heading to Toronto in two days, for a job at Chrysalis Records. I would intern for three months and secure new talent for the record label. Several of my duties would include marketing the talent, promoting the talent for local radio stations and making press kits for artists that are signed. I remember Ewan holding me in my arms and kissing me on my forehead ever so gently and urging me to 'make out' one last time before I headed out to Toronto. Ewan and I had been together for the past two years and met during our time at the University of East London. England was a place of great renown, awesome cathedrals, and a cobblestone-entrenched history. I enjoyed visiting the haunted castles and felt weary when I had to leave but I would remember fondly the beauty of the countryside and forever treasure the moment Ewan entered my life.

"Don't leave me Marianne," Ewan said, "you know I'll miss you".

"And you know I can't stay in England. I have a bright new future ahead of me and you know something, I deserve it," I exclaimed.

"Yes, you do. Only the best for you. You will visit me though, right?".

"Of course, I will. You know, I will. Now, you don't need to go home but you must get the hell out of here!" I said laughing.

"Alright, I'm going. I'm going. You have my number, right? And you'll Facetime me every week?"

"Yes. Yes. I promise to Facetime you every week and call you if you don't piss me off!"

"Ha Ha," said Ewan, "I could never do that to you!"

"You know I'll miss you and when my internship is over, I'm heading right back to England."

With that, Ewan kissed me one last time and left my apartment with a demeanor reminiscent of a child that doesn't want to leave their best friend's house. He glanced back one last time and I waved goodbye to him. I rushed back into my apartment and staring out my window, I made sure he made it safely back to his car. That was when I spotted the same man I had seen at the fairgrounds, standing directly across the street. He was staring at me intently, with a gaze that felt like a knife cutting into my flesh. I started to breathe heavily, and I quickly pulled my curtains shut. I was petrified. A man I had seen, only a few hours ago, was now standing across my apartment. I wanted to go back to the window to see if he was still there, but I was too scared. I made sure I locked my door and all my windows and headed straight to bed. I didn't want to believe that that man had followed me from the amusement park. All I did was stare at him for a few moments! Was he that peeved I had done that? I decided to wrap myself in my blanket and think nothing more of it.

The following morning, I had started to pack my bags in anticipation of my long-awaited trip to Toronto. I forgot about breakfast completely and focused on the long journey ahead of me. I remember thinking how long I waited for this moment. I was more than excited to start a new chapter in my life. I walked steadily to my window and very slowly pulled back the curtain. I had to be certain that the man who had been across the street, last night, was no longer there. I still could not fathom why this was happening to me but the last thing I needed was another traumatic event to turn my world upside down. My fear was that he would return tonight. My thoughts are suddenly interrupted by the sound of my cell phone.

"Hello".

"Hi Marianne. It's me Ewan. Umm…something bad has come up. Can I please crash at your place tonight?"

"Well, I don't know if that's the best idea. I mean I am packing up and getting ready to leave for Toronto. I only have tomorrow left to get prepared. Is there any other place you can stay for the night?"

"I haven't anyone Marianne. You are all I have. Please, I just need tonight to get myself together."

"Alright fine. But it will have to be just tonight. Tomorrow morning, you must be on your way!"

"Thanks so much babe. You have no idea how much this means to me. Bye"

With that I hung up the phone and continued about my day, getting ready for my trip. I later stepped out to buy roasted chicken for Ewan and I to eat in the evening. I went back home and spent the rest of the day relaxing, watching a movie and later taking a bath.

I must have fallen asleep in the tub because I was jolted by the sound of a knock at my door. Without fail, I then heard the door crash open. I slipped into my robe as quickly as possible and ran to the front entrance. I saw no one, nothing. I saw only that the door had been completely unhinged.

"Marianne. You should come with me, quickly!"

I turned to look behind me and it was the man I had seen at the fair. The same man I had seen the night before staring up at me from across the street was now in my apartment. He walked towards me, and I could do nothing but scream and run into the kitchen. My fingers fumbling through the drawer in search of a knife, I finally found one and, in my haste, cut my fingers. I shuddered at the sight of my blood. I almost fainted, when in the corner of my eye, I saw Ewan standing by the stove.

"Ewan," I cried, "help me please! Who is that man in my apartment? Please do something!"

Ewan walks over to me and without hesitating, strikes me across the face and kicks me, repeatedly, in the stomach. In agony, I no longer recognize the man I thought I had known for two years. Consumed by anger, my mind was at a loss to make sense of what was happening to me. I wanted nothing more than to ask Ewan why he was killing me. I could barely see the room as my blood mingled with my tears. I was convulsing and shrieking for help. Passing out from the pain, I thought I breathed my last breath. The last thing I heard were the sounds of heavy footsteps...the sound of blood-curdling screams from Ewan and the sound of his limbs tearing apart and falling onto the floor.

THREE

A Nightmare Unleashed

The throbbing pain in my chest was more than I could bear. Every time I coughed; my ribs ached uncontrollably. I had bandages wrapped around my chest and I was still wearing my blood-stained jeans. I found myself inside an unknown bedroom with gold chiffon curtains tapered by a crimson valance all of which were accentuated by green walls. On each side of my bed, was a nightstand: each with its own oil lamp. My bed was facing the door which upon a second glance, I noticed was ajar. I slowly inched myself off the bed with pain so agonizing I had to muffle my screams by biting my lip. It seemed to take forever to get from the bed to the doorway. I began walking slowly through the hallways; my mind pondering how I ended up here. Where was here? Whose home is this? The hallway stretched for what felt like a great distance. It wasn't until I was fully oriented that I realized I was in a mansion. I saw a window at the end of the hallway and made my way to it. Outside, all I could see for miles, was greenery. It dawned on me that I was in the middle of nowhere.

"Are you feeling any better?"

I turned around to see the man I had first encountered at the fairgrounds.

"Who are you?" I asked, "How did I get here?"

“I brought you here,” he said, “you were gravely injured.”

“Why didn’t you bring me to a hospital?” I replied.

“By the time, I would have done that, you would have died.”

“I don’t believe that!” I cried, “clearly, I am in the middle of nowhere. There is no hospital round these parts.”

“That is true,” he stated, “I performed minor procedures on you to stop the massive blood loss and thought it best to let you rest in my home until you felt better.”

“You do realize you have kidnapped me, don’t you?” I stood my ground firmly. “I could call the police.”

“That,” he replied, “will be of no use to you. I’ve been watching over you for some time Marianne and I wanted to protect you.”

“Protect me!” I was beyond confused at this point. “So, you brought me to your home, to recuperate, because you are that generous, of a person, as to help a woman you have never met before. And you are a doctor that can perform on-the-fly surgery. Have I missed anything?”

“That sounds about right. Except I’m not a doctor. Please Marianne, you need to rest. You haven’t fully healed. Take, as long, as you need.”

“I won’t take any more of your time. I am leaving right now. You haven’t the right to hold me prisoner. I’m leaving now and please don’t stop me!”

“I wouldn’t do that if I were you,” he said.

“And who are you to tell me what to do!” I yelled.

"Marianne, I understand this is a shock to you. You are not a prisoner in my home. Everything you need, I can provide to you. Everything you have, I have provided for you. You can leave when you have fully healed. Please just rest for now. Dinner will be served in three hours."

"I don't think you heard me well. I think you should clean your ears. I'm not staying here. I don't know you. I don't care about meeting you. You've kidnapped me and I have a trip planned in one day. I don't want to be here. Do you understand me," I was livid at this point. I wanted to hit him. "I am leaving and that is that." I pushed past him and pushed through the pain in search of the front entrance. I stood on the second floor, for a few moments, when finally, I saw the main entrance, of the residence, was one floor beneath me. I continued to walk down the hallway and make a turn to the right and saw two flights of stairs, ahead of me. I had to walk each step two feet at a time because my ribs were throbbing, but I didn't care. Once I reached the bottom, there were three hallways, one to the left of me, one to the right of me and one straight ahead of me. How was I going to escape this madness?

"To get to the front entrance, you must walk straight ahead of you, but I am pleading with you, Marianne, please don't go. You must heal and to do so, you need to rest."

"Well, you should have thought about letting me rest at a hospital!" I stammered.

"I told you, my child, I could not have done so," he mentioned.

"Excuse me, I am NOT your child!"

"I meant no offense to you. Kindly forget this notion of departing and rest for a few more days."

"You know, you really are something!" I yelled, "I'm going."

Before I could walk any more steps further, I started to vomit, and my head was pounding. I collapsed on the floor and trembled. I was trying to crawl, at this point, and wanted nothing more than to reach for the door. I moved a few feet in front of me, until finally, I could no longer take the stress of it all and closed my eyes. I lulled myself to sleep when the strongest arms I could ever imagine grabbed hold of me and carried me up the stairs. The warmth of the bed was welcoming against my back. And his hand cradling my head gently onto the pillow was pacifying. I felt as a baby and thought, I need to rest. As he calmly released me from his grip, I whispered: "I will make my escape."

"I'm sure you will sweet Marianne. Rest now."

The smell of white bean soup penetrated my nose like the scent of roses in a lavish garden. I was famished. I noticed my soiled bandages had been changed and I was now in a new pair of sweatpants and a blue T-shirt. My headache had ceased. On the left nightstand, there was a bottle of phenytoin. I've used this medication before to control my seizures. I've had them since I was a child and have had to learn to deal with them. I guess this mystery man was serious when he said he would provide everything I needed. If I wasn't injured, I would leave immediately. But I couldn't risk escaping in the condition I was in. When this man goes about his business, I will see to it that I find a weapon to protect myself. He cannot be home all day and surely there must be something in this house that I can use to defend myself.

I was still in agony but better than the day before. The smell of the soup was intoxicating, and it led me downstairs. I entered a luxurious kitchen complete with an island and cream-colored cabinets and a dining table fit for a king. Obviously, this mystery man has wealth beyond measure. At the table was the bowl of soup and I ate to my heart's content. I had only myself for company. I know this because after I ate, I walked through the entire mansion. I even went outside and surveyed the grounds. There wasn't anyone for miles around. For me to escape, I would have to hotwire a car if I could even find one. When I re-entered the mansion, I surveyed the hallways. The hallway to the right of me led to an expansive library. I sat myself on the couch and chose a random book to read. I didn't know what else to do.

"Was it a good read?"

I jolted from my seat. "Shit, don't do that, you scared me!" I shouted.

"Was it a good read?" he asked a second time, "did you enjoy your book?"

"Is that all you have to say to me?" I inquired, "you still haven't told me your name or why you've brought me here."

"My apologies. My name is Reagan. I should have introduced myself. Is everything to your satisfaction? Did you enjoy your meal?"

"Can you please stop with the pleasantries Reagan? You haven't told me what your intentions are with me? I want to leave."

"I can't let you go," he said resolutely, "I've explained this to you before."

"Why have you brought me here?"

"I want you to be fully healed before I tell you everything. It will come as a shock to you when I reveal the truth."

"What truth?" I stated firmly, "you can tell me now. I am ready."

"No, you are not."

"Reagan, please stop being so cryptic," I choked, "what is going on? I don't understand any of this. And what were you doing in my apartment?"

"Marianne, hush, child, I will tell you all in good time."

"Tell me now, please," I cried. My ribs ached when I said this. I had forgotten that Ewan's repeated beatings nearly destroyed my ribcage.

"Ewan…yes, he is quite the character!" Reagan said matter-of-factly.

"How did you know I was thinking of Ewan?"

"Marianne. There is much I know. I will reveal all, just not now. Please take this opportunity to heal and take whatever you need. I have everything you could desire. My home is your home." He cradled my face in his hands. I hated him. I wanted to end his life. All I was thinking was I did not deserve this.

"No, Marianne, you deserve so much more."

"How are you doing that? Stop it. I don't like it," I began crying, "I hate you. You think because you've taken care of me, I owe you something. I did not ask for your help."

"Please do not test my patience, my child. I will not tolerate it in my home and nor will you. If I wanted to hurt you, I would have by now. I only wanted to protect you."

"But I don't know you!" I screamed even louder with tears streaming down my face.

"Don't cry Marianne. It is not you. You are not so frail! I do know you and I have been watching you, for a very long time."

"Just let me go!" He looked me sternly in the eyes. I felt like a child being chastised by her parents for disobeying an unjust rule. And like that, Reagan turned away from me and walked out the door. He left me in the library, to wallow in my self-pity. I quickly ran after him but to my surprise, by the time I exited the study, he was nowhere to be found. I looked to the left and right of me and I saw nothing, no one. I ran down the right hallway and he wasn't there. I ran down the left hallway and still, he wasn't there. How did he move so fast? He was standing with me, but a few moments ago. I loathe this man. He is toying with me, and I'm disgusted.

FOUR

Irresolute Home

A rosary in hand, Marianne was falling yet again. She was crying out this time for anyone to save her. The sight of heading fast toward the ground made her heartbeat faster and faster. She knew she was going to hit the earth and like many nights before knew what horror that would bring. No! She thought, I can't go through this again. I don't want to meet my doom. I can't wake up sweating, irritable and frightened. Suddenly, she opened her eyes. The same dream that confounded Marianne was now a reality in her waking hour. Unlike previous incarnations of this lucid dream, Marianne had an unbearable itch on her back. She lifted her shirt and turned her back to the mirror and saw two tiny holes. It itched insufferably so Marianne rubbed herself against the door ledge. The holes were swollen, raised and red. She was sweating profusely and couldn't shake the feeling that her dreams were manifesting her wounds. This wasn't just a recurring hallucination; this was a warning. Marianne realized she had to make sense of her changes lest her changes control her. What was causing these changes? What continually brings them on? Marianne did not know the answers. Her new sense of purpose would be to find out why. "I am not one to back down," she thought to herself.

Again, in the late afternoon, there was a meal prepared for her in the kitchen. Again, she sat alone and retired to the library before the end of the day. Throughout the entire day, she was fatigued and inexplicably so. Her injuries still required much therapy, but she was recuperating faster than she expected. In just three days, she could walk without inching herself bit by bit, so why was she always restless and tired? On the one hand, she felt enhanced but on the other, she was in a perpetual state of weariness. Having to straddle between two opposing frames of mind and recurring visions of falling to her death made no sense to her.

Marianne retired to her bedroom, later that night but not before taking a knife out of the kitchen. She was going to fight Reagan when the right opportunity presented itself and she was going to win back her freedom.

****

"Hi. I'm Janice from Chrysalis Records. If this is Marianne, I'm calling to let you know we've been expecting you at our company for two days now. Last we spoke, you had made the arrangements to fly out to Toronto, but we haven't heard from you. We'd like to know if you are still interested in the position. Please call us back when you get this message."

"Marcus, what did I tell you? Marianne never made it to Canada. What could this all mean?" said Joan after listening to the answering machine.

"I don't know. We've checked all the places she likes to frequent and there's been no sign of her," replied Marcus.

"Look!" exclaimed Joan, "her plane tickets are still in her drawer. She never left the city."

"What has happened to her? She is not one to behave like this."

"I think we should go in search of her. We should try back at the university and see if she made plans to stay longer."

"I hope she's alright," said Marcus. The two of them left Marianne's apartment after searching every inch of it. They had been calling her, for the past four days, and received not a single reply. It was bizarre to say the least as Marianne was not one to ever disappoint her friends. Her apartment was in a disarray as she had not finished packing. Her furnishings alone stood in place.

"I suppose we should head out to Canada and see if she made it there by some other means. Yes, in fact, we should do that. Why don't I go to Canada, and you stay here in England a little longer," thought Joan.

"That does make sense," replied Marcus, "we would cover more ground and if I should encounter her, I could call you and let you know."

"Sounds fine by me." The two friends agreed to go their separate ways and begin their search for Marianne.

FIVE

SHELTERS OUTGROWN

It was 1 am in the morning. I decided it was best not to sleep. It had been three weeks since my capture and I needed to know more about Reagan if I wanted to kill him. I knew that I was alone during the day and every two or three nights, I would run into Reagan in the study or sometimes in my bedchamber standing by the doorway. He would stand there, looking at me, with a concern mirroring that of a father watching over his daughter.

I could feel his presence, she thought. I wanted to understand this, but it was beyond my desire as the pain from the puncture marks on my back consumed my every thought. I wanted to know why, whilst my ribs were healing, my back was hurting. I remember Ewan's attacks on my midsection before lying unconscious but the marks on my back are foreign. I often wondered why Reagan would stare at me until I fell asleep. I was disturbed by this but as the weeks passed, I grew accustomed to it. I assumed that Reagan wanted to make sure I wouldn't escape. I was tired of his surveillance. I wanted to rid myself of him. Sometimes I would just stare back at him and other times I would turn my back on him. He was beyond strange, and his vacant stare was horrifying. His eyes were a brilliant silvery-white with a faint bluish tinge. At times, when I would stare out my bedchamber window, I would find him prowling the grounds and catch him in the glimmer of the moonlight; gaunt, with sunken eyes, standing over six feet tall. His skin shone like alabaster and his hair fell loosely over his eyes. He had shoulder-length hair reminiscent of an ancient Egyptian hair style. He moved as though he were walking on air. It was frightful at times. He didn't seem human. I wonder what it must be like for him to keep up appearances. There was something odd about him. I do ponder if that's why he keeps his distance from me. No matter the reason. I must kill him, and I plan on doing something this very night.

How many more days have passed, I do not know. I stopped counting because my thoughts ran rampant about how to escape my fate. My fate which seemed, with each passing second, to escape my grasp. I did not know what I was up against, but I thought it best to die trying rather than remain a prisoner in his world. I knew only that he peered every night into my bedroom, gleaming at me from a safe distance; watching me for minutes only to disappear and then return periodically throughout the night. I knew this much because I could not rest knowing he was always lurking in the shadows. I slept sometimes, but every so often, I awakened distressed fearing for my life. Weeks had passed and tonight was the night, I would strike down my foe. I retrieved the knife I had hidden between the bed mattresses and placed it behind my back. I waited until what seemed like four hours had passed pretending my best to give the illusion of restful dreaming. Once my captor had left my sight, I proceeded to walk down the hallway. I crept slowly and peered inside each bedroom. I did not know where he was, and it never occurred to me to have followed him on previous nights to know of his whereabouts, but I thought it cautious to not do this lest he discover me wandering at night. Once I completed the hallway check, I proceeded down the staircase to the first floor. Again, I saw him nowhere. Again, I checked every bedroom and even looked under beds, and rummaged through closets. Never had I been more anxious in my life than I was right now. I was terrified he might appear behind me at any moment. My heart was pounding, and I could barely breathe. Following this search, I thought I could escape. I could run to the front doors and head to the gates and run into the forest in search of the nearest town. I estimated that no more than one hour had passed as I was searching for my captor's whereabouts. Defeated and exhausted, I could always turn back and head for my bedroom or I could take that chance and head for the front doors and make an escape. I will do it. It's now or never. I am heading for the front doors.

SIX

DELUSIONS OF GRANDEUR

This is it. I am standing before the front doors. I found my way by retracing my steps when last, I had collapsed from illness. I tried desperately to toggle the handle but to my utter shock, the door was closed. I should have known better than to think he would make it easy for me to escape. To my left, I saw two windows and grabbed a poker from the fireplace and tried to break the windows with it. I kept breaking the glass until, finally, it shattered and then I managed to break it entirely and jumped out the window running straight to the forest. At last, my harrowing nightmare is over. I need only run a few more yards into nothingness; into vast greenery and endless open space until city lights are within my sight. I kept thinking of my friends and the familiarity of their arms. My mind raced with delight knowing my prospects for the future would soon change. There was nothing I loved more than the cool breeze of the nighttime. It was a most refreshing change and soothing to my chapped lips and sore ribs. I can see now, distant lights, on the horizon. I will be home, I thought to myself. I will regain my freedom. There is no turning back. The adrenaline, pumping in my veins, carried my legs with each step despite the aches. I am close now; I can see two small lights in the distance. I must be near civilization and relief, my newfound friend, is beckoning me to feel elated once more.

Just a few more steps and I will reclaim my future; my destiny. So excited was I that I tripped on a rock but quickly regained my pace knowing that my life would be put back together again. I was running like the wind until I felt my shirt snag on a branch. I wrestled, for a moment, thinking my shirt would rip. I didn't care if I was stripped naked, I wanted freedom and could think of nothing more. I continued wrestling for a short while until I relented and turned around to tear myself free only to find my captor standing directly behind me. The shock and terror that was coursing through my veins was immeasurable. I was frozen in place. So rigid was I that I grew instantly numb; my throat closing in on itself, I couldn't scream. A tear fell down my cheek knowing my future was once again turned upside down. I could do nothing but stare into his eyes; hoping he could see my desperation and understand that I deserved my freedom. His stare was cold, desolate. I shuddered as more tears fell down my cheeks. What had I done to deserve all of this?

"Nothing", he replied. "You haven't done anything. It is not what you have done but what you will do."

I didn't reply. I just stood still and stared.

"You are coming with me. Do not fight me. Please."

This is it. I am going to do what I set out to do. I remembered suddenly the entire time I was running with the knife behind my back. Wide-eyed, I looked at him with disgust and spat on his face. He didn't move. I slapped him next. Again, he gave no response and again, he didn't move. I clenched the knife behind my back and impulsively, I struck the knife into his chest. I smiled when I saw the blood running down his shirt.

Now, I will run. Now, I will make my way back home. Just as quickly as I proceeded to turn around and run, he grabbed me around the waist and carried me over his shoulder.

"Will you fucking let me go?" I yelled. "Why aren't you dead? Please. Leave me be. Let me go!"

"That isn't possible", he said. "And I cannot be killed that easily."

"What are you? Why are you doing this to me?"

"I told you before I will tell you in due time."

"What does that even mean? You are cruel and unjust. I want out of this place, and I want to be as far away as possible from you!"

I knew he didn't care but yelling at him made me feel somewhat better.

"Marianne, please stop this. I cannot let you escape. Not now."

"Then when? Who are you to do this to me! I've been trapped in your home for days, weeks, and you haven't told me why!" I could feel my body going limp and falling into his grip. My body could no longer put up a fight as the aches had quickly returned. I was gradually falling asleep to the sounds of the rustling leaves beneath his feet.

"Please", I whispered. "Don't do this to me."

I could see now we were nearing the mansion. I was going to be put back into his prison. I hated him with every fiber of my existence. When I regain my strength, I will try again to escape. At least now, I know he cannot be killed so easily. At least I know, he is more than human. I am not going up against a crazed psychopath. I am going up against a force beyond my senses and beyond anything I could ever imagine.

SEVEN

REMEMBRANCES OF OLD

I sometimes remember how much I loved eating fruit and the smell of freshly baked bread and beer. I think I used to eat those things…once but very long ago. I long for those days when things were simpler. Now, I long for Marianne. I know she can help me, but she just doesn't know it yet. I remember that night I walked past her at Les Boutins nightclub with a gaggle of girlfriends. I think she dropped something, an earring or bracelet perhaps, and I retrieved it for her. She thanked me and continued about her evening. She doesn't remember but she had cut her finger on a broken wine glass. As she touched my hand, I immediately shivered at the sight of her blood. I looked at her and saw a million lifetimes in the blink of her eye. I know, after that touch, I drank her blood and I felt her then as I do now. I knew her in an instant and I wanted her. I admit I have been following her for a long time. I believe the Fair Folk refer to her people as sorceresses. A rare kind of human female that is highly intuitive and inter-dimensional, often, without truly knowing it. Such humans are the key to the coming war that my kind has and will continue to face unabated. So much of my kind have already died. I withdrew from the war because I cannot leave this earth; this plane without truly having lived once more. I have spent a millennium roaming Athens, Nairobi, the

Appalachian Mountains, Cairo, the Amazon jungle, every region of the earth and I have always waited patiently to encounter an anointed human being. They have no understanding of what is to come but I theorize that if I can bind myself with Marianne, in both this realm and the astral realm, an anointed witch, such as she, may be able to protect me against the ever-growing war between my kind and the cryptids. We are bleeding, each day, more and more, into the human world, corrupting their existence. For centuries, we have vowed not to interfere in human affairs. But as the war rages on, the veil that shields the human world shrinks. The thinner the veil becomes, the denser I will be, and I will perish for all eternity. This I must avoid at all costs. I cannot imagine not moving forward as the Great Shift occurs. If only I could convince Marianne that she is the one that will bring my deliverance. I cannot rely on my kind. I have been hiding in this forest for years and I wish not that the Elders find me. I have resigned my life to Marianne. She alone will take me away from my pain and she alone will resurrect whatever humanity is left in me. I will no longer be lost for she is my guiding light.

****

I awoke again sore but determined to strike a contingency plan. I will not allow this non-human entity to decide my fate. I remembered suddenly that I hadn't spoken to my friend Joan in weeks, possibly months now. I must find a phone and tell her to come and get me. Whatever foolishness my captor has planned, I will not fall prey to it. He caught me the last time because he must have been watching me the entire time. I must be more on guard. But then I thought, if he isn't human, how much more on guard can I be? I think I should play it safe for now. The best solution would be to get back into his good graces and slowly, methodically, manipulate my way out of his world. Yet still, something irks me. I feel as though there is a strange familiarity about him. It feels almost like déjà vu; like I have met him or know him from somewhere, but I can't quite remember. I struggle to make sense of this all. The best course of action now would be to play dumb. I couldn't sleep knowing my first plan had failed. I decided to walk downstairs to the study and read again.

"I didn't expect to see you here", Reagan stammered.
I was stunned. I stood immobilized, not wanting to encounter my captor so soon after my capture.

"I thought you were sleeping," Reagan continued. "I know you've seen me staring into your bedroom at night. I understand it unnerves you, so I no longer do it. Is everything alright?"

"The fuck it is. I hate you. I don't want to be here. Why have you targeted me? I want to go home!"

"I know you are frustrated Marianne. I think we should properly re-introduce ourselves. My name is Reagan. But you know this already. I have been watching you for some time now and I wanted to protect you from that man you think is your lover. He meant you harm."

"How do you know that?"

"I have been watching; observing you both for some time and the person who assaulted you was your handler; your controller. He was not your boyfriend."

"If you knew this, then why did you allow him to assault me."

"Had I intervened and told you I was watching you, all this time, and told you your boyfriend was a threat to your existence, you would not have believed me. I know for certain you would have called the police on me or reacted in some other similar fashion. Not that you would have succeeded in doing so but you would not have believed me."

"But he still inflicted harm on me, why didn't you –

"Because", Reagan interrupted, "that's the only way you would have believed me. I never wanted it, but I had to make you see; make you understand. Besides, I would not have let him kill you."

I merely looked at him, not quite knowing what to believe. I sat down on the couch, next to the bookshelf and just gazed outside the window.

"I don't get any of this," I replied.

"I hope to help you see the meaning of it all. There is a war going on Marianne and whether you want to believe me, it is happening all around you. You are a part of this war and you always have been."

"What war do you speak of? I can't bear to hear any more of this. I want this nightmare to be over. Will you please just let me go?" I was on the verge of crying yet again. I hated myself every time I cried.

"Marianne, I understand your tears. Shall I explain everything now? Are you feeling alright? Do you still get those recurring nightmares?

"You know of my nightmares."

"Yes, of course. I feel everything you feel."

"How is that possible?

"I drank your blood, Marianne. That night at the nightclub, I believe it was called Les Boutins. You dropped an earring or bracelet but you had, a few seconds before, cut your finger on a chipped wine glass. You were bleeding but only a bit, you were unaware of it. I handed the item back to you and when you grabbed it from me, some of your blood slipped onto my finger."

"I don't remember such nonsense."

"Oh, but I think you do. I think the memory is locked somewhere in the recesses of your mind. I was merely another mortal to you then so you wouldn't have noticed anything out of the ordinary."

"You said you drank my blood. What are you?", I blurted out.

"I think you know. I think you've always known."

"It's not possible. They don't exist," I yelled.

"I knew you would say something like that. Would you like to rest now?"

"Are you going to kill me?" I asked.

"No," he replied.

"Are you --

"Marianne, I think you should rest some more. I promise no harm will come to you."

"I ----

"Marianne, gather yourself and go to your room."

I was in shock. I did not want to believe the thing staring back at me was immortal. I felt compelled to do as he told me. I could not control my own body. What kind of power does he wield?

"My child, go to sleep now. And have sweet dreams. Let me know what you think tomorrow. May you rest carefree and without torment; so that you may answer my call and end my despair when the time comes."

EIGHT

COLLECTING LIVES

Only so much sunlight would penetrate the weeping willow. Dragonflies flew around me sheltering me momentarily from the sun. The rustle of the leaves was like feet moving about. The very shadows seemed to move as though the ghosts of the forests had decided finally to make an appearance. The breeze enveloped me, caressing me with invisible hands. Reaching up to the sky stood a three-pronged tree with limbs that curled downward stretching for the ground; needing desperately to feel the earth. The skies were blue and crystal-clear foretelling a future that has yet to unfold. The stream glistened under the influence of the sun reflecting its rays. I marched onward anticipating where next my path would take me. I knew only that my ignorance would be my guide. A butterfly greeted me under the bridge landing on my shoulder and then fluttered away but a few seconds later. In the distance, I heard voices and the sound of doors opening and closing. Houses stood atop a hill several feet away from the path I strode. I heard a police siren when suddenly I was thinking to myself "Marianne" and would she remember me still. The delicate balance of nature was in play and in full swing as evidenced by the one tree whose foliage had already turned orange. It stood alone from the rest as though making clear that its presence in the forest was not to be taken for granted. It had evolved, it was God standing still. In the blink of an eye, life can change so suddenly and the only justification for its change would be magic. Like people, we possess the ability to change into beings we thought we never could be. If only we could capture the secrets of nature and uncover Her magic; manipulating the energies surrounding us and becoming the sentient beings I believe we were intended to be. I must be strong and stand tall like the one tree whose foliage had decided to change before the rest. Further down the path, a father and son had been fishing, it seemed for many hours, hoping to catch something beneath the current of the waters. One cannot hope to catch life when it is forever transient. Life must first catch you. The fish swimming in the water would allow itself only to be caught if it so chose for although we believe ourselves to have power over nature, she alone will decide what is to become of our fate. We have forgotten it seems, having lost our childlike innocence, that without nature we shall cease to exist therefore must care for Her. Again "Marianne" crept back into my mind as I walked under the second bridge. The bridge carries me from one destination to the next and I believe Marianne to be the same. She gave me a reason to go on living and in spite of my petty attempts at winning her affection, it was her rejection that fortified my strength and allowed me to be reborn. She was the guide I had been searching for my entire life and I knew knowledge would not have been withheld from me through her. I changed and reflected on the demons I had so long wanted to exorcize. I felt liberated and began to see things take form like they had never taken form. Clearly, I could see the burning desire manifest out of my dreams and, like my journey on this path, my every move would be marked by virgin anticipation. I had a new purpose in life and nature, ever-changing, propelled me toward my newfound purpose. I have much to thank Marianne for...I wonder if she can sense my thoughts; I verbalize my thoughts always. Heading back home, I retraced my steps exactly. Like giant fingers crossing one over the other, the trees became my canopy. Seldom did my thoughts escape me. My mind could not relieve itself of yesteryear's transgression. Reminiscing was the only thing I could do best but how to shake those memories that perturb me still? How do I find the strength to accept my demons rather than subvert them? A leaf had blown and settled on my neck as though consoling me. The very spirit of the forest seemed to be pointing me in the direction I had, for so long, hoped for. I had the sense of being taken care of yet never knowing where next life would take me. I knew, my hope in Marianne, would be enough so long as I believed I could manifest her help in some way. Walking under the bridge, a butterfly addressed me yet again and landed on my left shoulder. Dragonflies flew above me. The shadows of the forest re-appeared, and the breeze came back again, sealing me within the confines of the forest. The three-pronged tree with curled branches were as limbs stretching downward, needing to go back to the source of its existence: the earth and like the butterfly that emerged from its cocoon, I too, have a desperate yearning to escape myself and return to where it all began.

****

Marianne closed her captor's journal. She found it hidden behind a bookshelf, in the cellar, when she had explored her residence, during daylight hours, weeks ago. This man not only had been stalking her for weeks, but he was dreaming of the day he would meet her. And verbalize to her what exactly? She was now not only afraid but curious too. "I am now a part of a world I know nothing about and whether I like it or not, I must search for my answers. Who or what is this thing that wants, no, needs me so desperately? I need to know so I can escape my fate and regain my sanity." Marianne tucked the journal between the bed mattresses and pretended to go back to sleep. She could hear footsteps heading in her direction and knew the immortal would once again return.

Nine

Tables Turning

Blood. Stains. Torn shirt. Joan's body lay lifeless on Marianne's apartment floor. Flies were circling her head. She had been dead for weeks. The police took photos of her body and were collecting all the evidence they could find. Janice of Chrysalis Records had called yet again pondering what had happened to Marianne. She involved the police and much to her surprise, the police discovered Joan's body in Marianne's residence. As a result of Janice's intervention, the police now have reason to search for Marianne. Ewan, Joan's friend, was called in for questioning but he was nowhere to be found. In fact, when they went to his apartment all of his belongings had vanished. The police now know that the last people to have seen Marianne were Joan and Ewan. With one of them now dead and the other missing, the police had more than enough reason to carry on with their search for Ewan and their search for Marianne.

****

Marianne was weary of her non-human resident. She had no idea what she was up against. The next morning, she went to the library but not to read. Instead, she stared for hours out the window and thought of every conceivable plan to make her escape…yet again. For a moment, she thought this is damned near impossible. I'm not fighting a simple foe. Maybe, she thought, I should re-read his journal entry about me and decode it for any hidden messages. Suddenly, from behind, Reagan entered the room. He stood still for a moment before speaking.

"Marianne, I hope you can forgive my capturing you. I need you for a great task."

"Yes, I know this now. I found your journal entry." I thought I might as well tell him the truth. A man of his power, I figured, I have no choice but to reveal the truth. I knew he could read my thoughts.

"I was looking for that," he said. "Do you wish me to explain myself? You may as well be told the whole truth. I am not in the habit of kidnapping women."

"Not in the habit of kidnapping women!" I proclaimed. "You shouldn't kidnap anyone. This is preposterous."

"I will need your help in the coming days, maybe weeks. And what I ask of you will be a great sacrifice on your part. But I implore you to help me. You are my last hope."

I could feel Reagan's stare piercing me even though he was wearing sunglasses. His stature was intimidating, and his very presence was like a spotlight shone on him wherever he went.

"If I comply and do as you ask, will you let me go?" I implored him. "Will this nightmare finally be over? And you will set me free?"

Reagan removed his sunglasses, and I froze in place. Seeing his eyes glare at my own terrified me. His eyes, up close, were like looking through a windowpane. Eerily, you could see right through them.

"Your eyes are...," I stammered to finish my sentence. I must have fallen into a trance because momentarily, I forgot where I was.

"Marianne, I need to know you can protect me when the time comes. Marianne, can you hear me? Marianne!"

I was shaken very hard until I snapped back to reality.

"What happened?" I said, "I felt like I had left my body but could do nothing about it."

"It's the glamour effect I have on mortals. I never meant to hypnotize you. I sometimes forget I mesmerize people. Do you forgive me?"

"Yes. I guess I do. What were you saying? I seemed to have lost my mind. What is happening?"

"Shh," whispered Reagan. "Someone has intruded into my home. Stay silent."

"What? I don't hear anything. Is someone inside?" I shrieked. "It must be someone come to rescue me!"

"No, don't be foolish Marianne. This person means you harm."

"No, it can't be! The police must have realized I have been missing for a long time and they've come to help me, at last! IN HERE," I yelled.

I heard footsteps on the upstairs floor, and I ran towards it as quickly as possible.

"No," cried Reagan. "Marianne don't go!"

I couldn't hear anything but my salvation upstairs. I knew I had an opportunity to escape, and nothing was going to stop me. I ran up the stairs and down the hallway to where I heard the footsteps and on the fourth door on my right, I saw Jacob. A friend of Ewan's from London. I was thrilled beyond words. I ran to Jacob explaining to him that I had been taken against my will and now was the time to help me escape.

I was about to jump into his arms when Jacob grabbed my arm and twisted it behind me. One second, he was standing in front of me, the next he was behind me. From the corner of my eye, I could see fangs protruding and without a moment's hesitation, he bit into my arm. I let out a piercing scream and bent over backwards in agony. I fell crashing to the ground and slumped into a stupor. I could barely breathe.

Smashing into the door, I could hear Reagan's footsteps. He gave such a hard blow to Jacob that he keeled over backwards. I could hear the two fighting but could barely move let alone scream again. I was too weak to move. I just let my eyes close. I soon fell asleep to the sounds of their battle.

"Marianne, Marianne, are you awake?" said Reagan. "Are you alright?"

It took me a moment to realize what I had been through. A flurry of pain in my left arm was reverberating throughout my body. I remembered now that Jacob had attacked me.

"Marianne don't be startled but Jacob tried to kill you. He must have followed you here."

I began to cry. This was the second attempt to end my life and I don't know what I could have done to bring this down upon me.

"Marianne, you have no need to shed tears. Jacob was Ewan's righthand man. He must have followed you here to my compound. I know you have no understanding..."

"Reagan, I don't deserve this. You have no fucking idea how I feel, how my world has turned upside down and how everyone I trusted has turned against me. Why am I being attacked? Am I a terrible person?"

"No, Marianne, you are not thinking clearly. You haven't done anything wrong, but you will do something bigger than you could imagine. Before I explain, I must share with you one other very important issue. Your friend Joan was found dead in your apartment complex in London. Jacob killed her. The police are now on the hunt for him and Ewan but having *disposed* of them both, they will soon realize their search for them will be in vain. Ewan was not human, like me. Neither was Jacob. If you allow me, I will explain everything, from the beginning and what the oncoming war has to do with you."

"Joan...is...dead." Tears streamed down my face. The harsh realities of my past came flooding back into my mind. My life is never going to be calm. It is never going to be peaceful. Every time I think I have found stability; it always gets torn away from me. I do not deserve good things, I thought to myself. I do not deserve happiness. I *am* a walking disease that attracts only the worst of people and situations. I must not be human myself.

"Marianne, my beauty, you are MORE than human. You just haven't realized it yet."

Ten

Origins

1022 A.D. In what is now called Mexico, a once great Mesoamerican culture that spoke the *Nahuatl* language once dominated the region. I was – what you call – a member of the Aztec civilization. At the time, we had *altepetl* (city states) and formed many political alliances and empires. I was a member of the *Tenochtitlan* state, and I was what you would call a chamberlain or steward, for the ruling king named *Kluktoani*. There were nine other kings at the time I was his steward. My duties included tending to his every whim, caring for his every need, and representing him before opposing alliances. I governed in his name and bore a peccary as an emblem and, always, warranted his authority. I managed the royal household as my father did before me. It was all I knew. I was happy to serve my king. I lived a relatively normal and happy life. Until, one day, as you may have guessed, my state had an altercation with an opposing political tribal party. They had kidnapped a handful of our people and held them as ransom in exchange for a portion of our land. We had, in the past, refused to trade with them because they reneged on many deals. Sadly, we went to war with them, and half of the captives were slaughtered. I fell in love with one of the remaining survivors. She looked very much like you Marianne. She had your eyes and your face and your hair. The first time I saw you,

I thought I was looking at her all over again and I began to reminisce about the past. I very rarely delve into my past, but you have triggered me to do so. I sometimes miss those times. There is a certain beauty in today's modern world, don't get me wrong. I love the "concrete jungle" as modern man puts it. I love the flower stands on corner supermarkets. I really enjoy your secular music. I often listen to the conversations of people in restaurants, and I have also enjoyed watching you, Marianne, for quite some time too. But I digress, when the opposing alliance went against my people, I was tasked to kill the leader. I couldn't do it, but I had to, or I would be sentenced to death. I beheaded the leader and my king sent raiders to demolish their lands. The memory of his killing haunted me for days, even months. But I was the king's steward and I had to do what I was told. I was certain that I would take my own life. The ordeal of taking another's life was something I had never experienced before. The trauma of it, cemented in my mind, forever sealed my fate. I blasted the king for his making me take a life and as punishment I was beaten almost to the point of death and forced into exile. The king would have had me killed but he thought it better to have me toil in my own thoughts, forever a wanderer, and lost to the elements. As I wandered further and further away from my encampment, I began drifting in and out of consciousness, from the heat. Exhausted as I was, I thought I was seeing things in front of me. I would blink and not see them only to blink again and see them reappear. I would see such things as palm trees, falcons, birds, waterholes, even my shadow moving ahead and away from me. I was beginning to think I was losing my mind. When the night drew close, I was enveloped fully in its darkness, and I would hear high-pitched yelping from afar and then very near to me. The sound would reverberate in my ear. At times, it would frighten me and at other times, I would simply ignore it. It grew in frequency, getting louder and louder until I could suffer it no longer. I yelled out asking what it wanted from me and what it was. Every time, I received no answer. I finally lost my mind and fell face first onto the ground. I think I wandered, at that point, for about a month, maybe two. My body gave in to hunger, fatigue, hallucinations, and thirst. I was going to die out there in the jungle but the yelping I had heard commenced once more. The shrieks grew painfully loud until I had to firmly seal my hands on my ears to keep from writhing in pain. "Be still" a voice said. "I mean you no harm." I thought I was hearing things again so naturally; I ignored it. I began praying to the ancient god *Tezcatlipoca* to change my fate and release me from my torment. Again, the voice spoke: "praying won't be necessary for I have come to bring you solace. Open your eyes and see my form. I am your god now and willing to change your fate. What say you my desolate one?" A shrill laugh emanated from her throat – yes, it was a woman's voice and again, I ignored her. I did not want to feel like I was hallucinating yet again. To be fooled, in that moment, was not something I was in the mood for. I just let myself sink deeper and deeper into my slumber until her voice was one in the same with the sounds of the forest. "AWAKE" shrieked the woman. She grabbed me by my feet and dragged me to a cave hidden in the depths of the jungle.

This was no place I had seen before. I used to wander in the jungle as a child, but I never strayed too far from the encampment. This was clearly a place hidden from all the tribes. It was like being thrust onto another continent and finding oneself, for the first time, in snow. Except this was not the north of Canada or the North Pole, this was a cave that was real yet not real all at once. "So many unchartered territories, you humans have yet to discover," she said. "So much to learn. You are but a child my beauty." I barely opened my eyes, that is, until she threw water onto my face and forced me to sit up.

"Who are you?" I asked.

"I am your rescuer," she responded. "I have seen you defy your king."

"I have done no such thing!" I exclaimed. "I killed a man to appease his honor. I am a coward."

"Nonsense," she replied. "You did as you were told, yes, but you felt remorse. That is most than any could ever hope for."

"What do you mean woman? You speak incoherently. I could have disobeyed my king and let him kill me. That would have been the better fate for us all."

"No! You did as you were told because you were simply following orders. You gave him several years of service and he repays you with ungratefulness! You felt remorse. You realized the error of your ways and confronted the king about it. You hated his decision, and he dismissed your sentiment! He was a fool. A good leader learns from his steward. A good king would rectify or find middle ground with those he is at odds with. He made you – NO – forced you to take another's life when he should have done so himself! He was the coward, and you were the victim."

I sat motionless listening to her words and let them sink in. She was right but I couldn't mouth the words to fashion the feelings arising out of me. I still took a life and I still had to live with that sentiment for the rest of my days. I wanted to hold myself and never let go. I began to weep and hang my head in shame. This woman…was right.

"Of course, I am," she said sternly. "I have lived for centuries, and I know better than anyone else how the human mind works. What if I could give you your power back and make you whole again? What if I could take your tears and alchemize them to saturate your face; revitalize your heart and change your fate!?"

I looked up into her eyes. Her eyes were red like the setting sun and her hair was wild and unkempt like a lion's mane. She was thin, very thin. She was pale and her veins shone clearly through her skin. She wore rags for clothing. The one thing she did wear that was both alluring and frightening was her smile. Whenever she smiled, I saw two fangs on the sides of her mouth. I was mortified. I had never seen a creature such as her. She was terrifying yet exotic all at once. My mind kept racing. Should I flee from her and make my escape? Or should I kill her then and there? I couldn't think straight.

"Then let me think for you, my sweet. Take my blood. It is the true elixir of life. Take your revenge. I will grant you the strength you need to free yourself from your pain. You can avenge your lover, you can avenge your father, you can avenge yourself. Be all that you can be and use my strength. Let me be your resuscitation; let me be your rejuvenation. I am everything there is and all you need to know. I have been for centuries, searching for someone whose will was as strong as yours, who can feel pain and grow from it."

"Are you going to kill me?" I asked.

"Quite the contrary," she said. "I am going to bring you back to life."

And with that she cut her wrist and poured her blood into a small bowl, letting it fill to the brim. She handed it to me imploringly and wiped away my tears.

"Do not fret my child. Drink and be no more afraid. Drink and release your pain. Drink and be forever changed."

I looked at the bowl for minutes just staring at it and wondered why I had deserved this fate. What had I done to bring this down upon myself?

"My love, shed no more tears. You haven't done anything. But you are about to do great things. Think not of what is happening to you but rather that it is happening *for* you. Your will is strong. You just can't see it. Drink from me and gather your strength. Be the change you know you are. There is a warrior inside of you. Embrace him and get your revenge!"

I looked at her, as a child looks at his mother and wanting to please this mother figure before me, I obeyed, and I drank. I felt the blood run through my veins and instantly something changed in me. I could hear my heart beating inside my head. I could feel each breath as though it were my last and my soul, as you would call it, leaving my body. It was surreal to say the least. I was transforming but into what exactly I did not know. Was I turning into the woman before me? Or was I turning into something else? In minutes, I had fallen asleep.

When I woke up, the woman was gone or so I thought. I felt pain in my backside and noticed I had clearly defecated the night before. I was not human. I was *something else*. I grabbed hold of the hammock that was strapped to two trees and unintentionally tore the hammock and uprooted both trees causing them to fall to the ground. I had inhuman strength, so clearly the woman had not lied to me that I would embrace her essence. This was jarring. I had to test what other powers I had. I began to run through the jungle and found I was running as fast, if not faster, than a cheetah. Or with the speed of say ten sprint runners combined. I could hear every sound of every creature, both great and small. I could see every creature in detail. I could feel the very air in between my fingers. It was like being born all over again. I was thirsty, however. I felt a thirst like I had never felt before. But I wasn't near any rivers or streams. I would have to leave the vicinity I was in and return to my encampment. It was next to the king's residence. I would have to confront him. I had the power I sought. I could make him suffer for the pain he'd caused me. I could make him pay dearly for his life and take the lives of his wife and children. I was a loyal servant of his for years and never once did I question his authority. Despite my thirst, I decided to make my way back home. Being exiled now meant nothing at all. I would take the king's life and watch his throne crumble before my eyes. The woman was right. There was always a warrior inside of me, but I was too afraid to unleash him.

Eleven

Renunciations

It took me a moment to truly appreciate what I'd just heard. This being, sitting before me, by the edge of the fireplace, just revealed to me that he is a vampire. I had my suspicions but I cast them aside because the thought of something preternatural existing was beyond my imagination. Of course, I have always had a fascination with the supernatural forces both seen and unseen that manifest themselves, in our world but never would I believe that I would see the day that a being such as Reagan would manifest before me. It's safest to relish in such desires on the movie screen or delve into the recesses of an author's lavish machinations in a novel. Better such beings exist in our artistic creations; our nightmares and dreams.

"Marianne," whispered Reagan. "Will you help me?" I stood still processing everything I had been told. How can I help a being such as he? I am merely human.

"I don't know how to help you because I don't know what you expect of me! You still haven't explained what this war between your kind and those other beings entail."

"Marianne, when the time is right, you will awaken a higher being that resides both in and outside of yourself. I don't know what power will awaken inside of you but when you become more so fully yourself, you will do things you could not possibly imagine doing right now. When the cryptids come for me, as they always have, you can shield me, perhaps even save me."

"I still can't get over the fact that you are what you are," I stammered. "How can I be sure you won't turn your back on me once this war is over?"

"It's never over Marianne, it only stagnates, often times appearing to dissipate but the fight will go on for as long as there is a world for it to thrive."

"Why don't you show me what you truly look like? Why can't I see you for what you really are? After all, if I am going to help you, I may as well know what you are."

"I haven't shown myself to you because I did not want to frighten you! I knew that if you would see me, for what I really am, you would run for dear life!"

"Well, I am only human, after all. And what if I choose not to help you. What then?"

"I would only go seeking for you. You do have my word Marianne that once this is over, I will leave you be."

"Hmmm…isn't that what they always say?! For all I know, once this is all over, you will kill me. No sense in fighting back, you would overpower me every chance you get. Show me what you are Reagan! I need to see. I need to know!"

Reagan sat still pondering what I believed would be my reaction to him. He resolved, at last, to show me his true appearance. He stood up slowly from the chaise lounge and removing his sunglasses and leather jacket, he walked over to me, taking care to step lightly towards me with each movement. He seemed to float. He was always so graceful; so surreal. He stood now five inches from my face. Still, statuesque, immobile and changeless, he looked down at me with what appeared to be glassy, see-through eyes that glimmered with a reflective surface. I could see every vein on his face. His flesh appeared hardened, pale with a greyish undertone. He had a look of despair and despondency. He was ugly yet captivating, sinister yet remarkable. You want to be pulled into him but you are repulsed all the same. I did not like what I saw. I muffled a scream because standing so close to me, his face was overpowering and menacing.

"You fear me," Reagan stated. "You can't stand the sight of me."

"Reading my thoughts again," I retorted. "Yes, I cannot deny you frighten me but I would rather see you for what you are then not know at all." After a long moment's pause, just staring into his ocean-deep grey eyes, I said: "please continue with your story."

Reagan just peered right back at me, not moving and not breathing. This was all so unreal. It was like a revivified corpse, on the brink of dying, and clinging to the last vestige of life.

"Alright," he finally responded. "The woman I had fallen in love with, I still longed for her. Once I escaped the confines of the forest, I headed back to my compound searching for not only revenge but for her touch as well. The vampiress who made me disappeared. I was overcome with stupor. I was still learning of my new self and still testing the limitations of my powers but my mind had not yet fully turned. There was still an inkling of humanity left in me and I felt that the unification of my body and soul with the woman I loved, would enliven what little hope and zest I had left for life. I wanted to be in her arms and be with her and for me, that was all that mattered. If only she could love me and see past my hideous form, I would still have a reason yet to live. Once I managed to gather myself, I was able to find my way back and hiding a good distance away from my tribe, I tried looking for her – Nebuelah (that was her name). I found her half beaten and taken prisoner by our nemesis. My instinct was to save her first and then seek vengeance on the king who betrayed me. She still held so much beauty in her eyes despite her scars. My plan was to sneak behind the enemy lines and tear them limb from limb, one by one. I could do so stealthily and speedily – this much I knew. I had my newfound powers to my advantage. Rescuing my love and vanquishing my king would be nothing short of easy. I found Nebuelah. She was sitting by herself tied to a tree. The now opposing tribe had been beheading people, one by one. I moved swiftly and headed straight for the tree and using all of my might, I broke Nebuelah's chains and grabbed hold of her. She turned and screamed at the sight of me. She was mortified and it hurt me to no end. I had to stifle her screams because I did not want the advancing party to see the two of us making our escape. I pleaded for Nebuelah to see past my appearance. I tried telling her that it was I, the man who loved her. She kept struggling. Her kicks came with such fury but she inflicted no harm upon me. I told her to look into my eyes and to see the man she once knew, hidden beneath the corpse-like appearance. But I was nothing more than a zombie to her. She hurled rocks at me and when she realized it inflicted no damage to my head, she fell to the ground aghast. She said I was not human and she would run back to camp to warn the others of a demon lurking amongst their people even if that meant her death. She could not see past my outer shell. I was foolish to think my love for her would move her to accept me in any shape or form I took on. I yelled out to her that I loved her and she turned to face me. I begged one last time that she believe it was me, the man who fancied her and wanted to be near her and hold her for all time. She stood still, simply looking at me, then slowly approached me and let me envelope her in my arms. She returned to me, even though she was frightened and helped me despite my hideous facade. I understand now that I had an immature view of love back then. Love does have its limitations and how one appears is how one is perceived. Love cannot reach outside this material realm. It cannot fathom outside of what one was taught. I, no longer human, ceased to be love's recipient. In that split second, I held her thinking something in me forever changed. She saw in me what little humanity I had left. Suddenly, she fell to the ground, her eyes half-mast, rolling up into her head. She had been struck by an arrow. Someone must have heard our commotion and sent a search party for us. I squeezed Nebuelah as she screamed. I held onto her while she lay motionless on the ground. I told her I loved her and she looked up at me in a daze. She whispered my name and with her last breath, she asked me what had happened to me and why did I look so strange. I was shocked for only in her last moments did she recognize who I was. I hurled a scream unlike any other and that's when the armies headed in my direction. It took me no time to battle every soldier coming onto my path. I was maddened and lost in a sea of grief. I tore every man I came in contact with by tearing arms, legs, slashing throats, and ripping out vertebrae. I was decimating the tribe. I was going to leave no trace of any one person breathing. The grounds would be red with the bodies of everyone who stood in my way and my anger. I would not rest until my vengeance was satiated. Before the night was over, I must have killed hundreds. I gorged on blood and felt delirious and peaceful all at once. I had no clue that drinking blood would provide such clarity. It was then and only then I realized what I was: a bringer of death, a harbinger of doom, one whose existence was predicated solely on stripping the life source of others. Today, you humans call us vampires. But we were evil spirits back then and to a rare few, we were gods. If I was to exist by taking the lives of others then I would do so by killing those who vexed me, those who vexed others, and those whose sole purpose was to bring death and destruction wherever they went. For if I was the harbinger of death, then death I shall be to those who bring it. Before day break, I heard a stifled moan. My preternatural ears could hear the moan more than five miles away. I ran as fast as I could to the sound only to discover it was Nebuelah. She had somehow survived the bow and arrow attack even though it penetrated her stomach. She was kept prisoner by none other than the vampiress who made me. She took it upon herself to imprison my love. This was my final test. If I hadn't been through enough already, I was now going to go through my greatest ordeal.

"The prodigal son has returned to me," she yelped. "Do you want to reclaim your lover?"

I was stunned. Why had she kept Nebuelah for herself? Why was she imprisoned by the very person who stripped me of my humanity?

"Because I needed the right catalyst to set you off."

"What do you mean," I responded.

"I knew how much you loved her. If I captured her, I knew you would be angered to destroy all the tribes, including your own. I needed a blood bath and you delivered it right to me!"

I was beyond reproach. What had I done? To witness the deterioration of my one true love in front of my very eyes was the most painful transformation I had ever undergone. It did not even come close to my newfound vampiric nature.

"You must be wondering why I had done this to you! Let me tell you my sweet. For a millennium, I have roamed the earth and sought solace. After so long, I desired peace. But before I return my body to the fringes of the earth, I must pass my wicked gift to another. In you, I saw the greatest potential there ever was. One who was so loyal, one who was so faithful, one who loved his master like no other. In you, the greatest empath ever my eyes beheld existed before me. For you see, I know what you do not know, after existing for so long, that such a person like yourself would never have his love returned to him. A person, such as yourself, would never have been given his due rewards for a lifetime of service, care and love. Empaths seldom ever receive anything in return. Your kindness was beyond human capacity, it was supernatural…almost angelic. By making you a creature of the night, I insult the Creator. For tainting the purity of one so true, the insult to God is even greater. To corrupt his most loved creation, a man of pure heart, is to vilify God. In you, I have found my release. I can take my life and depart from this plane knowing the Dark Gift of vampirism was given to you. And to further blemish your soul, I will take the life of the one you love so dearly. Your precious Nebuelah."

"No, not Nebuelah! She hasn't done anything to you!"

"She need not do anything to me or anyone for that matter. With her death, your heart will be eternally broken. You will only know despair and your soul will forever belong to the Dark Lord; the one who lives in the recesses of your mind, body and spirit; the one who lives beneath!"

"You cannot do this. I have done you no wrong. Nebuelah has done you no wrong. I implore you, let her be."

"I have spared three soldiers. They will do what they please with Nebuelah and ravish her body. They must obey my command for they are under my control. This is my final gift to you. To ensure your vampiric conversion, I will make you watch your lover's destruction!"

"You cannot be serious. Are you mad woman? You are of the devil! Yes, you are! Leave her be!"

I then ran to Nebuelah to grab her by force but the elder vampiress' strength was far superior to mine. She thrust me twenty yards up into the air with her mind. I landed on my back and had the wind knocked out of me. For a moment, I lay still, semi-conscious and my right leg had broken. I turned to my right and saw the men seize Nebuelah. One of them, to my horror, was my king. The man I had been a steward for, for all of my adult life. He stripped Nebuelah naked and had his way with her. I could not move as I watched in horror, the pain he inflicted on her. The other two men held her down while the king punched, choked and slapped her repeatedly. She bled profusely from between her legs and I screamed every time she did. She was turned over on her back and the king had his way with her again. At one point, she passed out from the pain. I screamed Nebuelah's name over and over again and told her everything would be alright. I would be next to her and rescue her and save her from her doom if she would hold on just a little longer. My leg was finally beginning to heal. It was a sight to behold. I was looking at my fractured bone put itself back together and the tendons, ligaments, muscles self-heal. It was like watching a seamstress stitch a garment together and like fabric, the many parts of my leg, re-attached itself to my thigh. Once healed, I sprung up and ran with all my might and headed straight to Nebuelah. I don't know how but my rage was in control and I managed to hurl the vampiress into the air. I then headed straight to the men who had their way with Nebuelah and broke the arm of the man to her right and slashed the throat of the man to her left. As for the king, he was still atop Nebuelah and I gave him the worst punishment of all, I ripped off his genitals, and then I sucked him dry until every last drop of blood had drained from him and then I crushed his spine and sucked the marrow from his bones. I wasn't even thinking at that point, I was pure animal. Nebuelah was barely conscious when I turned and looked at her. I walked over to her and leaned over her battered body. "Nebuelah," I whispered to myself. I heard her whimper and moan. Her lips moved; I believed she wanted to say something but couldn't. I held her head in my hands and kissed her forehead. I felt her right arm reach for my hand and she opened her eyes half-mast and stared into my own. I thought I heard her utter "help me" and I responded that I would. Unfortunately, for me, I did not know that my vampiric blood, at the time, could heal the human body if given on the brink of death. I lifted her into my arms and carried her away with me. The vampiress blocked my path.

"Your initiation is complete."

"Move out of my way woman!" I shouted.

"But you cannot have her. Nebuelah belongs to me!"

"The hell she does. I will destroy you woman. Let me have what few moments I have left with Nebuelah or I will break your heel, break your back, and twist your legs!"

"Now that's the spirit. Rage and fury. So much of your life you have wanted to feel glorious power over those you kept watch over, provided and cared for. Your king, who chose Nebuelah, for a fourth wife was yet another woman betrothed to him. How dare he take one so beautiful from you! This must have hurt you deeply. Show me how you truly feel. You must be relieved that you no longer have to serve such a vile man!"

"Nebuelah had nothing to do with this. Leave me be!"

"Nebuelah is the last part of you that is human that needs to be destroyed. You cannot love humanity for you are no longer human. Let go of this woman that upon seeing you in your present state wanted to kill you! Is that true love? Wanting someone to see past your hideous state?!"

"Yes, but you made me this way! I did not ask for this. If you turned me into what it is I am now then surely you can turn Nebuelah! She and I can be together forever in this monstrous state."

"Why? So, you can condemn her to your endless state of suffering?! I CHOSE you. I did not choose her. I have been watching you for so long and I knew inside of you a hungry wolf resided. It pleased you to kill the king, didn't it? Nebuelah is nothing. She is meaningless. You cling to your mortality. It weakens you."

Suddenly, Nebuelah spoke with a shudder and she said: "Kill me please. I can't live like this."

"No. Don't say that!" I exclaimed. "I can still save you. How will I go on existing without you?"

"Please," she said. "Just kill me. I am in so much pain."

"Do it," said the vampiress. "End her suffering so you can end yours!"

And without fail, Nebuelah went limp in my arms. I screamed for what felt like hours on end. And then nothingness. I dropped to the ground on my knees and still holding tightly to her, I sank my teeth into her neck. I drank her dry. And the taste of her was delirium itself. You cannot imagine what it tastes like feeling the ebb and flow of the human spirit as it slowly dissipates moving from one part of the human body to the next starting with the feet and ending at the crown. She was in me forever but not as I wanted her. It was maddening looking down at her dead body. It was lunacy.

Yes, I admit now I hated the king. I despised his policies. I knew, in my heart of hearts, that Nebuelah was never going to be mine and I felt that for all my years of kindness to others that I was not receiving my just rewards. I can admit now I was bitter and resentful of those around me. I wanted more out of life and the vampiress must have snuffed this out of me. She knew how I truly felt and that weakness – that weakness alone – is how I fell into her grasp. For you see, the living dead can always sense a blackened heart. That is the very gateway through which they enter our world. She was right. I could not argue any further with her. She knew what was in my heart and in my mind and she tethered me to her by way of my darkened thoughts. I wanted revenge and I wanted it hungrily. As much as I loved Nebuelah, she was never really going to be mine. And that's why the vampire always wins! The vampire always knows what weakness lies behind your eyes. That is his true skill. That is his real glamour. That is his true calling. I let Nebuelah's body rest on the ground and with my last ounce of strength; still shaken by the battle, I used every fiber of my will to move swiftly from Nebuelah's resting place to the vampiress' face and without hesitation, I slashed her throat with my fingers, punched and ripped out her guts and broke both of her arms. With her last breath, she looks at me with the most devilish smile and says: "thank you for releasing me. I have waited for this for centuries my dark prince. I no longer have to roam the earth a former shadow of myself. I am free."

And finally, it was all over. The one who made me was now dead. I was a pawn in her game and I played right into her hands. That was the test and I failed. She knew of my heart's impurities and she played upon that feculence to unleash the monster that was always dormant in me. I gave her her sweet release and she gave me mine.

Twelve

Longing Sentiments

It took me a while to grasp the levity of the story I had just heard. I was motionless just thinking of the depravity Reagan had been through. It was unlike anything I had ever heard. I could feel a shift in the air between us. I wondered if it was painful for him to relive those dreadful moments. He had lost his home, his way of life, the woman he cherished and his very humanity simply because he was the target of something beyond his comprehension. The weakness that had dwelled in his heart was the very personification of the vampire's existence. Our deepest fears, anxieties, resentments and hopelessness are the root cause of our evil. The reason we exist is to heal ourselves and to heal others; to eliminate the weeds of self-destruction lest we allow evil to be the bane of our existence. It all makes sense to me now. There was clearly something in me that Reagan was more than merely attracted to but attached to. The resentment I harbored for others whose lives I perceived were inexplicably superior to mine; easier than mine; more peaceful than mine; more serene than mine, I hated them. I may have overcome much to be where I am but I still despised those that did not have to overcome the hardships I had to overcome. I was most definitely not without fault. So much hidden rage left unprocessed, Reagan was attached to that black hole and that black hole was the key to unlocking the power within me. Only time will tell what power lay buried within me. I stood silent just staring at Reagan. He was looking outside the window. I did not know if I should speak to him. I was petrified of him though mysteriously drawn to him. Is that the power vampires wield over us, simpleton humans? I suppose that is how they capture their prey. After all, it is so much easier to entice one's victims. Reagan stood absolutely still. It was incredibly fascinating how still he stood until he disappeared from my sight.

I got up off the chaise lounge and moved towards him never dropping my gaze from him.

"Reagan," I said. "I'm sorry for what you've been through. It must have been horrible."

Reagan turned his head very slowly in my direction. He just stared at me with a gaze so penetrating, I thought my skull would break. His eyes were so deep, so grey like an overcast afternoon sky. They were eerie. I think we just looked at each other for a solid minute or two, not saying a word. Reagan, finally, broke the silence.

"Rest Marianne," he said. "You need to get some rest."

"Reagan," I answered. "That's all you ever say. You only ever tell me to get rest. Please, if there's anything you'd like to share with me. I'm here. I'm listening. I really do feel bad about everything you've been through. Your story is…is…well, I guess I'm speechless. I'm sorry I remind you of her. I can't imagine what it must have been like when you set eyes upon me. But I'm not her. I mean…if you want me to be her. If that's what you need, I cannot provide that for you."

Reagan, as he was about to exit the bedroom, turned to face me in the doorway.

"Marianne. I could never ask anything of you that you could not do. You need to rest because danger is imminent. I can sense they are near. They are coming for us both and you need to get ready."

THIRTEEN

REAWAKENING

I don't remember falling asleep. I awoke at 3 am in the middle of the night in search of Reagan. He must have gone out hunting. I couldn't get his story out of my mind. I replayed the events over and over. I felt a kind of pain I'd never felt before hover over me. It was like a dark shadow had claimed my soul and I was lost in a sea of never-ending abyss; dark and deafening; maddening and tormenting. I stood, by the window, waiting for Reagan's return. I then decided to walk myself downstairs to the kitchen and I prepared myself a glass of water. I heard a chair shuffle to the right of me and I thought I saw a shadow moving in the corner of the room.

"Can't sleep."

"Oh my god!" I yelled. "I didn't know you were there Reagan. You frightened me. What are you doing in the kitchen?"

"Why can't you sleep?" he replied.

"Well, to be honest, I can't get your story out of my head. I just keep playing it over and over and over in my mind. What was the world like when you were human? Do you think I am a descendent of Nebuelah? How much do I look like her? Do you still have feelings for her? Have you ever been in love with anyone else after her passing? Have you made any more of your kind? Do you regret anything? Are you…"

"Stop," stated Reagan matter-of-factly. "What does all this matter to you?"

"It doesn't really. I just wanted to know more about you. I am stuck here with you, at least for the time being. I just thought that maybe…we could…get to know each other."

"I don't see how that will be of any benefit to either of us."

"Well, I do see the benefit. You expect me to help you, don't you? I think if we took the time to connect and understand each other better, maybe, this power of mine that lays dormant will be that much stronger. I need to know who you are, here and now, so I can help you. You do want me to help you, right?"

"I will need your assistance yes and as promised I will let you go when you have performed your task successfully. But I care nothing for you personally. You need to sleep. Please be on your way."

"You're always telling me to get rest or go to sleep. You're constantly telling me what to do and how to feel or react. You know what you are? You're a piece of shit. I think you should go fuck yourself Reagan. Don't tell me I'm stronger or better than that. And don't you tell me that I'm not speaking as a woman should. I'm not from your bloody time! In fact, you know what Reagan, you can piss off! I'm not helping you in your stupid quest to save yourself. I'm leaving."

"YOU CANNOT LEAVE ME!"

"I can do as I please you FREAK!"

Reagan, in the blink of an eye, was standing before me. It was like he teleported. My breath was knocked right out of me. He quickly grabbed hold of my neck and was choking me. He slammed me against the wall and pulled me up off my feet. Tears were streaming down my face and I was struggling to grab hold of something, anything to steady myself. I gradually felt nothing and closed my eyes. I could feel myself slumping in his grasp. It was like free falling and just waiting for the moment of impact when I would hit the ground.

"Please," I pleaded. "Reagan...please."

His grasp was getting tighter and tighter until finally I passed out. Everything went black.

****

When I awoke, it was 11 am the following day. I saw bruise marks on my neck. I couldn't quite speak. I just kept coughing up blood. Reagan obviously meant to kill me. I was left confounded by last night's events. I think I sat on the bed's edge for an hour before I headed downstairs. The fact that I was not dead after standing up to the vampire fiend means I must be really important to him. I don't know how much more I can test his limits. I will avoid Reagan as much as possible. I don't want to do what he asks but I also don't want to die by his hand. I know what damage he is capable of. I must make a stand. I broke one of the wooden legs of my bed and decided I would use it as a stake.

"Marianne," blurted Reagan.

"Wait...what are you doing up now? It's daytime. I thought vampires slept during the day."

"Marianne, you have to move quickly and come with me now. They are outside, headed in our direction. The cryptids will barge through the front door."

"What? Tell me what is going on. I demand to know!" I shouted.

"I am over a thousand years old, so the daylight does not affect me as it would a young vampire. Now, please, come with me. There is a tunnel beneath this castle and we can make our escape there. It will give us just enough time."

"I'm not going anywhere with you."

"Fine. Then I will have to carry you."

"Don't touch me you MONSTER!" That's when I pulled the makeshift stake from behind my back and plunged it into his chest. Reagan stumbled but only for a moment. He immediately pulled it out. And he gave me the most baffled look.

"You've clearly watched too many movies! A stake was not meant to kill vampires. It only keeps them in place and even then, that does not work. Stop your foolishness. To think you thought a stake would stop me."

"Well, I am only human."

"Indeed, you are."

"Screw you, Reagan!"

That's when suddenly a creature of enormous size barged through the door. It had the head of a dog and the body of a man. It stood nine feet tall. It had the stench of rotting flesh. I was petrified. It ran across the room faster than my eye could see. It carried a silver blade and stabbed Reagan in the stomach and he fell backwards. But just as quickly as

Reagan was penetrated, his wound healed. It was instantaneous and unlike anything I had ever seen. That's when the creature looked in my direction and came stomping towards me. I was terribly frightened. All I could do was scream when suddenly a forcefield half the size of the bedroom emanated from my body. It threw the creature into the air and away from me, his body slamming into the wall. That's when Reagan stood up and looked directly at me and said: "that's your gift, you can generate force fields with your mind."

"What's that?" I stammered. "I didn't feel anything. All I know is I was screaming."

"Let's head for the tunnel," he replied.

Like a child, I followed him. I wanted nothing to do with that creature.

"Reagan, tell me what's happening," I pleaded.

"The tunnels first and then I'll explain."

I grabbed hold of his hand and he pulled me with him as we headed down the basement. Once there, Reagan led me to the cold storage room where a hidden door was located. He pulled it open and told me to run in first. I did as he said.

I just kept running until I could no longer breathe.

"Marianne, you have to keep going."

"I'm tired. Please let me rest. I can't run as fast or as long as you can!"

"Then I will be forced to carry you."

And carry me, he did. We headed straight into the open fields, some ten kilometers away from the estate. He put me down gently on the grass and I looked up at him and waited for his command.

"I'm sorry," he said.

"For what?" I replied.

"For choking you the night before."

"Oh that. After seeing that frightful creature, I had completely forgotten about that. It's water under the bridge."

"Do you forgive me?"

"There's nothing to forgive."

"You know I would never kill you."

"Yes. I know".

"I am still in love with her. I, sometimes, long for her."

"For who?"

"For Nebuelah. And yes, you remind me of her. That is one of the reasons why I followed you around."

"I shouldn't have pushed you to answer so many questions. After all, vampires do keep their identities secret."

"Will you forgive me for what I'm about to do?"

"What are you going to do?" I asked.

"Only this," he replied. That's when Reagan pulled me closer to him and very gently, he held my hand and kissed it. "My real name is Esuahway. That was the name given to me at birth. Sometimes, I remember my past and sometimes I don't. Nebuelah, among other things, comes and goes. I often black out and don't remember who or what I am and sometimes I can't even make sense of the world around me. When I saw you, in the dance club, I saw Nebuelah in your eyes. And you reawakened something in me that had been dormant for many centuries. I don't like to speak on such things."

"How was it?"

"How was what?" Reagan said.

"My dancing, in the nightclub."

Reagan just stared at me dumbfounded.

"Reagan, it was just a joke!"

FOURTEEN

PRIOR ENGAGEMENT

Deep in the forest, away from the city, all was lost to Reagan and I or should I say Esuahway and I. I hadn't bothered to ask him if I should address him by his true given name or not. The last thing I wanted to do was vex him. I followed him to the water's edge. We were headed to the north of England. England, I thought to myself, and then suddenly I remembered I had a job prospect in Toronto. With everything that had been going on, I completely forgot about the new life I had made for myself. Had it not been for this preternatural being, I would have been in Canada taking on new ventures and meeting new people. It's funny how in the blink of an eye, your life can take a turn for the strange, the worst or the better. I only now remembered my girlfriend who must be worried sick about me. Esuahway was leading me to a catacomb hidden deep within the earth. He explained to me that the cryptids often reconvene in that area. They had many tunnels running throughout the entire planet; one always connecting to the other and many a battle were fought between vampire and cryptid, demon and slayer, witch and Fair Folk of all kind unbeknownst to the human world. Sometimes, innocent humans would get caught up in the wars but for the most part, humans remained ignorant of what lies beneath the earth and what often times, lies right in front of their eyes. In the case of "awakened" humans, like myself,

Esuahway explained, we are targeted because our power is so great that we can affect many a great change in humans and supernatural beings alike. Sometimes, humans would participate in the great wars and take sides. Depending upon the attachments they made, humans would side with demons for glory, power, or wealth. Other times, humans would side with Fair Folk in exchange to leave behind civilization and more often than not, humans would side with vampires in exchange for immortality. Vampires, demons, fairies, cryptids, will often seek out such humans to aid them in their quest for dominance. The wars have been going on since time immemorial. Modern humans came into existence long after, so these beings kept their existence a secret from humans knowing that if they were to gather in great numbers, they could eliminate them into oblivion. As time progressed, and more and more scientific discoveries were made, these beings made an oath to further hide their existence knowing that the scientific community could unravel their existence and truly obliterate them from the earth. Esuahway was turned during the Aztec civilization; approximately one thousand years ago as he so clearly stated and humans, during his time, feared vampires and many worshipped them. Now relegated to the TV screens and magazines, the pop musicians and dance club scenes, vampires have no purpose in a world that consigns them to the world of fantasy, fiction and romance. Except Esuahway does not glitter, and he is not the least bit sexy. He is frightful. The glamour ability vampires possess enable them to seduce their prey. It is quite similar to the toxoplasma gondii that cats emit so that you feel compelled to feed and pet them.

It's effective as it allows the vampire to do the least amount of work possible to ensnare his or her prey. You see past the vampire's demonic appearance: grey, decaying, empty, and fearsome. Fortunately, for me, my awakened ability allows me to shed my mortal "trapping" and see past his appearance, at least for some time. He had been in battle with both witches and demons and this time, with cryptids. Devilish creatures that are half-human half-animal hybrids infused with demonic blood. Esuahway had slaughtered an entire clan of dogmen when they raided his home for mingling with one of their kind. He had taken the blood of their victims to escape the torment of having to kill humans. The cryptids often hunted human hunters who went camping. They also killed any human who knowingly or unknowingly killed one of their own kind. And finally, those wanting to end their own lives or those who became lost in the woods, would find themselves kidnapped, tortured and then killed by these creatures as well.

"I'm tired. Do you mind if we stop for a moment Reagan or Esuahway. I honestly don't know what to call you."

"Call me anything you wish. I assume many identities as the times change. But we must move forward, we cannot stop for anyone or anything."

"Esuahway, please. I'm only now discovering my powers. Creating that forcefield knocked the wind out of me. My head and my stomach hurt. I just need a moment to breathe. Do you mind if we camp for the night?"

"Alright."

I was positively stunned. It was the first time he had ever agreed to do anything I asked.

"Surely. You know I am still human. I don't have the strength, speed or agility you possess."

"That can change shortly. The stronger you grow in your powers, the greater your strength."

"Where will we rest?" I asked.

"We can rest right here."

I lay down on the grass and let the blades tickle my feet. I removed my shoes because my feet were sore and I removed my jacket because I was burning up. I sat up against a tree making sure to keep my back erect. I looked up at the night sky. In the forest, the stars are plentiful and highly visible. You don't see that in the city. It was refreshing to say the least. I had no means of contacting my girlfriend. In our haste to escape the clutches of our fiend, I neglected to call my girlfriend. However, what awaits me next won't require a phone. Whatever my girlfriend is thinking, I hope she doesn't go looking for me. I wish I could warn her but I can't.

"Are you thinking of your friend," asked Esuahway.

"Yes. Are you reading my thoughts again?" I replied.

"No. You just have that look of someone who is worried sick about someone else."

"I just hope she doesn't go looking for me. It's not worth the effort. I wish I could tell her what is going on but she wouldn't believe me."

"I am sorry I choked you, Marianne."

"Are you still on that? You have nothing to feel guilty about! The bruises on my neck healed nicely. I suppose it's one of the advantages of having this power of mine."

"I meant I don't harm women unless of course…"

"They are evil like that vampiress that turned you! Reagan…I mean Esuahway, you don't have to explain anything to me. If you help me get through this ordeal, I will help you get through yours. These cryptids or monsters or whatever they are, they are coming after you, aren't they?"

"Yes. They raided my home when I was living in the southern United States. I would feed off of the remnants of those they kept prisoner, many of whom were humans obsessed with the preternatural or the unusual. I encroached on their territory. But truthfully, I grew tired of hunting for humans myself. It was just easier to feed off of the human remains they left behind. I wanted nothing to do with their…"

She's asleep. The poor girl has fallen asleep. Her head has sloped to the right. She looks so uncomfortable. I think I should lie her flat. Yes, I will lie her down gently, flat on the ground's surface and cover her body with my jacket. Her legs are so soft, so smooth. Her skin is flawless. She has the most beautiful eyelashes, so lush and so long. Her hair is a bit matted but that's understandable given everything she's been through. I want to hold her close to me. I want to whisper in her ear. I want to feed from her like I did, back at the mansion, when I would gently bite into her back. I forgot to tell her I sometimes did that in her sleep. Her taste is unlike anything I have ever consumed. Should I hold her close to me? Yes, I will pull her close to me. I don't know how to tell her the truth. I don't think I can. She will hate me when she learns the truth. She will think me a monster. She will kill me. She will hate me for all eternity. How can I tell her that she ***is*** Nebuelah?

FIFTEEN

The Battle Begins

"Wake up Marianne! You must wake up now!"

"What's going on?"

"The sun will be rising soon. We must head for the caves. We have the advantage of daylight."

"Esuahway, I don't feel well."

"Marianne, please. You must get up."

"I'm being serious. I feel terrible. I don't think I can join you."

"Sit up. Let me see you clearly."

I sat up and looked at Esuahway, my eyes still half-mast. I felt limp. My feet were tingling.

"Marianne, I know this is hard. You may feel like all you want to do is sleep. It is simply the changes your body is undergoing that makes you feel that way. I understand it is frustrating. But for now, we need to move."

"Alright. Alright."

I held onto Esuahway very tightly. I was half-dazed and half-awake and I gripped onto the back of his jacket with all my strength.

"Stay close to me."

"Of course," I said.

He led me into a cave and deeper still until we were in the catacombs. I believe we were beneath the Cheviot Hills or at least that's what I thought I heard Esuahway say. We were at the border of Scotland. I was finding it quite difficult to see in the dark.

"Let your eyes adjust. Breathe. Take your time."

"Alright. Esuahway, may I ask you a question?"

"Yes."

"Were you holding me last night, as I slept?"

"Yes."

"Thank you."

"Sshh. I can hear those same creatures you fought back at my compound. Stay with me Marianne."

We stealthily approached the creatures. Esuahway told me to be ready to fight. I just looked at him dumbfounded. Me? Fight? I have never been in battle. And I only accidentally created that forcefield because I was scared.

"I'm scared."

"I'm with you. You have nothing to fear."

The creatures were tall, grotesque and quite fearsome. I was breathing heavily and my heart was pounding. I could barely hear myself think. I would even forget to breathe, at times. My eyes were watering. They were itching me beyond measure. My stomachache was getting more intense. I felt like emptying my bowels.

"Esuahway, please we need to slow down."

"You can't! Just push through your pain Marianne. I need you. I NEED YOU!"

"What is going on with you? Why are you so upset?"

"I can't let what happened to me in the past happen again. I need you now more than ever. YOU CAN'T LET ME DOWN!"

"I swear you get stranger and stranger with each passing day and what do you mean by what happened in the past?"

A cryptid must have heard our conversation because suddenly one of them was charging towards us. Esuahway pushed the creature sending it flying in the air. This alerted the rest of them that intruders were in their midst and we were, in a matter of seconds, faced with two dozen of them! They were going to attack us and we had to think fast.

"You can do this! Don't let me down Marianne."

"I hope not!" I stammered.

The creatures were moving fast. They had incredible speed and stealth. I summoned all of my strength and manifested a force field that surrounded myself and Esuahway. He would knock them down, one by one. Sometimes, he would slash a throat, sometimes he would break a spine and at other times, he would break their legs. He was quite a sight to behold when he fought. Clearly, he is not someone to mess with when angry. The force field protected our bodies should any of those fiends attempt to touch us. It gave Esuahway the advantage he needed to get close to them causing maximal damage knowing they caused minimal damage to us. They were in awe, so much so, that they commanded another legion to attack me from a hidden part of the catacombs. I was giving Esuahway the protection he desired. This fumbled their plans to take him out and take him out they wanted very much. So much so, their fervor knew absolutely no bounds. One of them hit me in the back of my head and for a moment, I lost focus but quickly regained my composure when I gave a kick with such fury that the creature fell backwards and tumbled into other members of his clan. I was feeling myself being drained. The reprieve I yearned for finally came in the form of Esuahway's beheading of the last cryptid. At last, our first battle is won.

"Now, what do you mean by what happened to you in the past can't happen again?" I looked at Esuahway with imploring eyes.

"You," he replied. "You cannot be lost to me again; a second time."

"I don't know what you mean."

"I lost you a thousand years ago and I can't lose you again Nebuelah."

To say I was stunned was an understatement.

"You aren't Marianne. You are ***my*** Nebuelah."

SIXTEEN

ESCAPE TO DANGER

I ran. I ran faster than I've ever run in my entire life. Speed was one of my enhanced abilities now that I have embraced my newfound powers. When I could afford to lose his gaze, I left Esuahway in the catacombs of northern England, and headed back the way we came. I ran so much I could barely see the trees as I fled. Everything around me was a blur. Thankfully, I memorized the nearest road closest to the mansion I was kept in. I decided to keep going until I was standing by the nearest highway. I would flag down a vehicle and demand to be taken to the nearest city. It was surreal how quickly my feet carried me away. At times, I felt I was floating on air. Once I reached the highway, I began flagging down cars. Fortunately, one vehicle pulled to the side of the road and I was let in. I told the driver that I needed to get to the nearest city to meet someone urgently. Of course, this was a lie but I was not about to divulge the details of what I'd been through. If there is one thing, I learned from being with Esuahway, it was to trust no one. The driver proceeded to drive me as quickly as possible. Heading southbound, we eventually passed a gas station and a small suburb close by. I pleaded with the driver to let me out, as this was the nearest city and this destination would more than suffice. Instead, he continued to drive speedily and ignored my pleas to stop. I yelled at him and demanded he stop at once but he refused.

"We haven't reached our destination," the man proclaimed. "Marianne, you are my destination."

The man suddenly pulled up by the side of the road and horrified, I saw before my eyes, a cryptid. It was the same being I encountered at Esuahway's home. The demonic dogman reached for me in the back seat. I kicked him back with my feet and unlocked the side door to my right. I headed straight for the forest. The creature followed me and to my surprise, was as fast if not faster than I. I ran in zigzags to lose him but he was cleverer than I expected. He leapt over my head and landed directly in front of me some ten feet away.

"Stop running my pretty. I could eat you for a meal!"

"Get away from me," I yelled.

"You really thought you could get away from us!" the creature said.

"I don't even know who the hell you are."

"Esuahway was right to search for you. You will do nicely to help in our cause."

"I'm not helping you or him. I'm not helping anyone."

"That is YOUR problem. Come with me my dear."

"No!"

I ran back the way I came and headed for the car. I thought if I could get in the car, I could drive myself to safety. But the creature anticipated my move and leapt in front of me, pushing me back, causing me to stumble. He then grabbed both my feet and dragged me away. I was trying to grasp at anything to stop from moving. But his grip was supernaturally strong. My head was getting bruised from the rocks beneath the earth. I was struggling to breathe. I was screaming and screaming just waiting for the moment to end.

Then suddenly I heard a yell from the creature and saw his head flying above me in the air. I turned around to see what was going on and to my relief, it was Esuahway. He had decapitated the creature.

"What were you thinking? Leaving me?" he shouted.

"What was I thinking? What the hell were you thinking? You called me Nebuelah last we spoke! I know exactly what is going on. You're a crazy man who can't get over his ex and for some odd reason, you think she's me! You need to get your head straight. You need to get your shit together! How dare you kidnap me and use me to live out your fantasy of some woman in an era gone by! Ever since I've met you, everything in my life has gone bad. I've lost my friends, I've lost my job, I've lost everything I've worked hard for. I FUCKING HATE YOU!"

I walked away and left him standing there. I was going to head back home and forget about everything that had happened.

"Wait, Nebue…I mean Marianne. You don't remember me because you've lost your memory. The cryptids have the elixir that will restore your memory or at least I think they do. That's why I fed from their human remnants. I wanted to map out their caves to find the hidden elixir and then you and I could finally be together."

"Wow, you really are good. You make up the most incredible stories. How desperate you must be? I'm leaving."

"Please Marianne. You don't understand. This happened centuries ago. Your memory was wiped clean and I had to bring you back to me. It's happening all over again. I can't lose you a second time."

"Do you even listen to yourself?"

"Marianne. I know it's hard to understand. But I need you to see."

"To see what? Reagan or Esuahway, or whatever, just leave me alone. Maybe you should let this woman go. This woman, you once loved, she's past. You can always find someone else. You can always move on. Why is she so important to you?"

That's when Esuahway looked deeply into my eyes. He looked like he was about to cry.

"Alright," he stammered. "You can leave. I won't…I won't go searching for you. I suppose you are right. Maybe I should just move on."

Blood tears began to run down his face. It must have taken every ounce of strength for him to say what he said.

"I will take you to the city and you can depart for home. Your home."

He walked away silently. His feet were afloat. I somewhat hated myself for the way I spoke to him but I wanted him desperately to see things from my point of view. There is something amiss. There is something he is not telling me. Maybe it's too painful. Maybe it's some kind of unfinished business.

"Follow me," he said.

"I will," I replied. "Reagan…I mean Esuah…"

“It’s Reagan,” he said. “What is it?”

“I didn’t mean to hurt you. The way I said the things I said. I only meant that I think you are hurting yourself by not letting go.”

“Marianne. I was wrong to kidnap you and to push you into something you clearly weren’t ready for. When the time is right, and there will come a time when all will be right, you will be the one to seek me.”

SEVENTEEN

FALLING HOME

He left me at the airport with my belongings with a one-way ticket to Canada. I would call my friend, Joan, and begin my new job in Toronto. Esuahway did not look at me once when he dropped me off at the airport. He let me out of the vehicle without so much as a blink of the eye. I didn't know quite what to feel or say. I let myself out and headed for the terminal.

I walked steadily toward the gate but something inside me was pestering me. I felt an uneasiness in my stomach. I tried my best to ignore it and decided to push forward. Was I really meant to live an ordinary life and get a career like everyone else? Or have I been assigned a deeper, more profound purpose in life? Was Esuahway right? Or was I letting his words control my mind? I've always felt like I didn't belong in the world. I was always subjected to the harshest realities more than anyone else I had ever known. But to what end? For what purpose? It's strange but being away from Esuahway made me feel even more uneasy with myself than I had before meeting him. A part of me wanted to return to him but I thought to myself I only felt that way because I had gotten used to him. It was weird not being with him. I had never felt a longing like I have now – in this moment – not being with him. Was he right? No, of course not! Get yourself together girl! Don't put aside all you've worked for, for a man you barely know! Remember: he kidnapped you! He violated you! I must forget about him and look toward a brighter, newer day.

I approached the airport attendant and handed my ticket to board a one-way flight to Canada and let the airport staff check my bags for security purposes. I walked past the turnstiles and headed straight for the plane. I was to enter the walkway and board seat C18. I went to my seat and waited patiently for the other passengers to get seated. I placed my handbag in the above compartment. Shortly thereafter, a man sat next to me. He had long black hair and bushy eyebrows. He had a permanent frown on his face and was quite tall. He sat to the left of me and proceeded to stare at me. I felt quite uncomfortable. I ignored him and continued staring straight forward. I started to breathe heavily. To say I was worried and scared would be an understatement. I just assumed he would stop but he didn't. I wanted to ask what his problem was but thought it best not to engage with him.

"You are coming with me," he said. He had a knife to my throat and a maniacal smile.

"Please don't kill me," I said.

"Come with me and I won't."

"What do you want with me?"

"Do as I say NOW!"

He quickly took my handbag from the overhead compartment and shoved it in my face. He then grabbed my wrist and told me to stand up or he would stab me in the gut. I did as he said.

As we left our seats, a flight attendant asked if we needed any help and my captor replied that we did not and that there was a sudden change of plans so we could not fly to Canada at the moment. The flight attendant explained that it was a shame we could not journey to North America and then explained how we were to process our refunds online. My captor begrudgingly said "thank you" and proceeded to nudge me in the back to exit the plane.

I could feel the knife in my backside. I tried walking a little faster, hoping to begin a run but my captor caught on to me and held me back from moving any faster. We exited the airport and he shoved me into a car. I could feel it already – we were heading back to the catacombs. The place I had dreaded I was now heading back to but for what purpose I did not know.

Once we arrived, I was told to climb the mountain. Instead of heading deep into the caves, this time around, I was going to the top of the mountain with my captor. The walk was long to say the least. It was dreadful and I despised every moment of it. He continually nudged me as I headed higher up the mountain. I sometimes slipped and he was certain to catch me every time. Clearly, I was not meant to fall. I had a higher purpose for this being who now, upon a second glance, I noticed resembled the dogmen I had encountered earlier. At the airport, he was human. It is clear that these beings could shapeshift when they pleased. To think of how long they have existed among humans without anyone becoming even slightly aware of their kind let alone their numbers is astonishing. Esuahway had said they existed thousands of years before humankind came into existence. Seeing them in person, I believe him to be right.

"If you must know," said my captor. "Earth is only an illusion; a mirror of another world. Our kind come from that other world but that is not your concern."

"You can read my thoughts!" I proclaimed.

"Yes. You should be so careful to shield your thoughts every now and again."

"Why are we headed up the mountain?"

"You'll see, my dear. You'll see."

I tried to calm myself by breathing slowly. I steadied myself with every step I took. Once I was at the top, I was told to hold a rosary. I was in disbelief, I stopped breathing. This was just like my dream or rather my nightmare. The recurring nightmare that I was falling whilst holding a rosary was coming to pass. It was a warning the entire time – and much too much for me to take!

"Please, whatever it is you are about to do. Don't do it," I pleaded.

"Shut up!" yelled my captor.

Below I could see dozens upon dozens of dogmen. The entire clan had gathered at this very spot to watch my demise. It was all too clear to me that I was being watched the entire time I had left Esuahway. I was swimming in fear. My mind was racing. I wanted to run away but couldn't. The only way out of this was down…down to my own death.

"With Nebuelah's death, we shall never be conquered again. For she holds the key to our destruction!"

"What," I shouted. "I am not Nebuelah! Who is this Nebuelah? I am not her!"

"Silence woman!"

My captor struck me in the face. I fell to the ground but was immediately pulled back up.

"We will push Nebuelah to her death and her destruction will bring forth a new era for our people where we shall rule and no creature, vampire or demon, witch or warlock shall destroy us! For Nebuelah is the key. And with her death, the door to our annihilation shall be locked forever more!"

The crowd below me cheered. I was bewildered beyond belief. This was it. This was my nightmare come true.

"KILL HER! KILL NEBUELAH."

The crowd was chanting my death, over and over. I was crying and the tears would not stop flowing. I was nudged to the edge though I tried not to be pushed. Once I was at the very edge of the mountain cliff, I was shoved so hard that my left foot gave way and I fell onto my right leg.

"NO. PLEASE. I'M NOT NEBUELAH!!!!"

And with my final plea, going unheard, I was pushed off the mountain and I screamed what I knew would be the final scream of my life.

EIGHTEEN

LOVERS PAST

1020 A.D.

"Quickly, we must run from here!"

"Why?"

"We don't want the king to know what we're about to do!"

I held Esuahway closely in my arms and I wouldn't let him go. I wanted to ravage him there and then. He held my gaze as he always had with purity, innocence and rapture! I never wanted someone more than I wanted him. He was everything I had hoped for and everything that I needed.

"What are we waiting for?" he said. "Let's get to it."

We held back no more. I was eager for him to be inside me and I would let him have his way. We made love for hours. We were living a dream; a paradise unlike any other and the secrecy of it all made us all the more ravenous for one another. We would lay still for a long time until finally, we fell asleep in each other's arms. I loved his strong hold over me. I didn't just feel protected; I felt empowered. His strength inspired me to be strong myself. He always made me feel like I could do anything.

Suddenly, there was a knock on the door. We quickly woke up, scrambled to put on our clothes and slip on our sandals.

"Let us in!" yelled the servant. "The king requests your presence Esuahway. You must give counsel for the next tribune."

"Yes," he replied. "I am coming."

"Nebuelah, you must escape through the back door. Don't let anyone see you slip out. Remember, I love you."

"I'm sure you do," I said. I kissed him on his forehead and made my way to the back door. I had to be careful and not let anyone see me leave his quarters. I was to be the fourth wife of the king. And if word got out that I was with the king's steward, I would be executed.

"Please open the doors. The king needs your presence immediately!"

"Yes. One moment." Esuahway watched me slip through the back door and run back to camp. I looked back briefly to see him open his door and let the servants in. Then, I ran and went back to my people.

"Please enter."

"The king needs your assistance with the upcoming tribune. Our rivals want to acquire one third of our lands for their weapons artillery and use it as a defense quarter against their enemies. We must vote and decide if we should share our land for a price or annihilate the idea altogether. Furthermore, we must prepare Nebuelah for the king's upcoming wedding."

"Nebuelah!"

"Yes, Nebuelah. Have you seen her as of late?"

"No, I haven't. When will the wedding take place?"

"In a fortnight. Is everything alright? You seem distracted."

"Oh yes, yes. I am alright. I have been preoccupied with other things is all."

"Well, focus now Esuahway. We must depart now for the king's quarters. He requires your assistance."

"Yes. Yes. Let us go."

I walked behind the king's servant absent-minded. I was thinking only of Nebuelah and my love for her. I could barely get anything done constantly worrying about her and not wanting her to get caught for our affair. I could never lose her and I knew that I would be lost to this world forever if she were no longer a part of my life.

As we entered the king's quarters, to my dismay, I saw Nebuelah sitting next to the king. She was being fitted for wedding garments handpicked by the king himself. She had a look of despair in her eyes. She turned swiftly to her left and saw me standing before her. She almost stumbled but I caught her.

"How are you Nebuelah?" I stammered.

"I am fine."

"You will make a fine bride."

"I suppose I will. Thank you steward." Nebuelah bowed before me and took her place next to the king.

"Nebuelah, my beautiful, please leave the steward be. He and I must speak on matters that pertain to our kingdom. The division of our land is of the utmost importance."

"Yes, your highness," she replied.

Nebuelah looked at me with sorrowful eyes. She would watch me constantly throughout my conversation with the king.

"Nebuelah, will you get us water, please," asked the king. Nebuelah rose to her feet in search of water. She returned with mugs and water in hand. I grabbed hold of the mug and touched her hand as she handed it to me. She gazed into my eyes and almost spilled the water.

"Nebuelah, be careful, are you trying to bathe the steward?" said the king.

"No, your Majesty. I was not. I will be more careful next time."

"It's alright, your Highness. I could always use a bath every now and again." I looked at her lovingly and wanted to caress her but held back with all my might.

The king and I resumed our conversation and every once in a while, I would look to Nebuelah and catch her looking into space; pondering her fate or briefly looking toward me and then quickly looking away. She knew not to incur the king's wrath. She would be executed and this I knew all too well. I would never allow such a thing to happen to her, of course but until we could devise a plan of escape, we would have to – as you say nowadays – "play our cards right."

We ended the conversation with a bow. We decided to split the land with our rival tribe under a few conditions. They would pay us an annual tax. They would have to remove themselves from our quarters when we saw fit and they would have to lend their artillery with us if and when war broke out. They were not entitled to our women. They were not entitled to our armies. And they certainly would not be entitled to our throne. They would be watched by our guards round the clock and if they should ever stand against us, they would be destroyed.

The rival tribe agreed to our terms and together we forged a new alliance. After the meeting, I quickly headed back to my quarters because I knew Nebuelah would be waiting for me there. We always met up close to midnight and slept till the break of dawn, at which point I would safely send her back to her camp with her people. Night after night, we would resume the same routine. It was our unique circadian rhythm of love and our way of letting each other know we would never give up on one another.

Nebuelah was my own true desire and my sole mission in life. She was everything to me and I would stop at nothing to have her.

****

1022 A.D.

After I killed the king, I went back to my home to retrieve some of my belongings. But upon entering, I could see the silhouette of a woman in my doorway.

"Nebuelah, Nebuelah!" I cried.

"No. Not Nebuelah."

I did not recognize the voice. Another woman was in my domain.

"Who are you?" I yelled out. "You are in my home. I command you to leave immediately!"

"No. Not until you give me her!"

"What do you mean, foul creature!"

"Your sweet. Your love. Your precious Nebuelah."

"What do you speak of? Nebuelah is dead."

"Really?" said the foul being.

From the shadows, emerged the demon. It was a creature like no other. It was the vampiress I had encountered in the forest!

She was holding Nebuelah by the neck and had long talons for nails. She was going to slash her throat.

"How could this be? I thought I killed you! How did you come to possess Nebuelah's body?" I pled with all my might. "Let her be!" Nebuelah was crying. She was also in shock and very petrified.

"I remember how you plotted against the king. I remember you desired his would-be wife Nebuelah! I remember having read your heart, you wanted his throne as well! As for my resurrection, silly boy, I am IMMORTAL! I retrieved Nebuelah's body, shortly after you buried her. She still had some life in her left and I gave her a pint of my blood to reanimate her! I want you to witness her torture all over again, for your ridiculous attempt at ending my life!"

"If you give me your Nebuelah," she said, "I will make you king."

"Why must you want Nebuelah!" I responded. "What is she to you?"

"She is everything I desire to be, young, beautiful, strong, and MORTAL. With her sacrifice, I will have my connection to this new age to ensure my survival! I will make her mine!"

"Take me instead. Take me. Leave Nebuelah be! I am stronger and older."

"I take what I desire and I desire Nebuelah."

"Please, I beg of you!"

And without hesitation, the vampiress bit Nebuelah on the neck and began sucking her dry. I ran as quickly as I could and tried pushing the creature aside but she flung me across the room.

"STOP IT!" I yelled. Nebuelah's eyes were half-mast, she was being drained and losing consciousness. It was at that point, that the vampiress slit her wrist and fed her from her. Nebuelah was not aware of what was happening. She had her head tilted back and her jaw forced open to take in the blood. It was at that moment that I went for the creature and pushed her aside.

"You fool!" stammered the creature. "If I don't feed her, she will die."

"What do you mean you foul beast? How can you feed my Nebuelah your putrid blood?"

"Because, my blood is the source of eternal life!" The vampiress punched me and moved swiftly from me to Nebuelah and resumed feeding her her blood. Nebuelah drank the blood and slowly began to regain consciousness. She briefly reawakened and then collapsed to the floor.

"NEBUELAH! You damn creature, you killed her. I will end your life NOW!"

"Try if you can!" laughed the being.

I ran towards her, ready for battle and about to give her the biggest blow of her life when she suddenly dissipated into the air. She vanished without a trace.

"Nebuelah," I cried. "Can you hear me? That demon is gone. She has departed. Wake up my love!" But Nebuelah was gone. She was no longer breathing. She lay so still. It was terrifying. I have seen men lose their lives in battle but to see someone lose their life the way Nebuelah had was jarring to say the least. A creature STOLE her life. A creature STOLE her essence. A creature STOLE her blood. And I allowed it to happen! I was as guilty as the demon.

I had taken Nebuelah's body back to her camp. I explained to her people, the very few that remained, that she was brutally attacked by a stranger on her way home from the king's court. They did not take my word even though I was the king's steward and despite the fact, she had just been at the king's court. Nebuelah's people wanted vengeance for her death and they felt that annihilating my people was a just recompense for the king had destroyed most of their people, many decades ago. I pleaded with them, again, that her death was the work of a deranged stranger. They did not settle for such an explanation. They believed my king's army sought her death, for the army secretly believed she was a witch (and was indirectly responsible for past failures in trade with other tribes) and in so believing, they took matters into their own hands and purged one-third of my land, of its people, resources and livestock. This was horrible. I wanted to let people know there was a monster in our midst who may have killed more people, not just my precious Nebuelah, and that we have been placing blame on one another for far too long. This creature must have been killing for years, decades maybe even centuries. I could not know. I would be taken for a fool if I told everyone that a blood-drinking fiend, non-human, fierce and preternatural, existed among us. I had to let the war play out though my soul bled at the plight of it all. My heart was forever broken, my people imminently lost and my belief in what I knew to be true, was now forever gone. There are many things that go bump in the night, and the vampiress was one of them. I would stop at nothing to find her. Capturing the monster was my new mission in life. I would end hers the way she altered my Nebuelah's and hang her head for all to see.

****

Yet again, I was witnessing the stillness of my loved one's body. She lay broken and dead for a second time. The cryptids were cheering at the sight of her body. All they knew was that she had the blood of the Elder vampiress who had attempted to end my life centuries ago. Marianne was too strong to exist. The blood within her could exterminate their entire species. For this reason, Marianne was hunted. I wanted to save her and yet, I failed again. When the cryptids had dispersed, I went to the bottom of the cave and carefully grabbed hold of Marianne's body. Her legs were broken, her neck too. She was mangled beyond recognition. She was not the beauty I had beheld only days before. I took her body with me back to a motel off the highway. I explained to the motel attendants that she was my wife and she had gotten drunk at a bar and I was charged to carry her home and let her rest. They did not suspect a thing. I booked us a room and lay her body gently onto the bed. I slit my wrist and placed it on her mouth, parting her lips ever so slightly. I let the blood flow into her. I watched it go down her throat as I held her head up. I gave her only so much blood as I was hungry myself and needed to feed. I locked all the windows and drew the curtains. I barricaded her in the room. I sealed shut the front door by twisting the handle inward using my strength. No one was going to enter Marianne's room until she was fully healed. And my blood, I am sure of it, would do just that. Marianne still had not woken up to what she truly was. And it certainly will be no easy feat to tell her once she fully heals. I only hope and pray that her body is restored to its full rigor. She needs to know who she really is. I am depending on it. Marianne – Nebuelah – you will always be my one true love. I only ask that you can find it in your soul to love me as I do you.

NINETEEN

Human No More

When I awoke, I was in the worst pain I had ever felt in my life. This was far worse than Ewan who had pummeled me in the gut or when the cryptid had twisted my arm. I looked down at my legs and screamed in horror. They were broken. My neck was extremely sore and strangely enough, it felt as though it had been twisted all the way round my back. Suddenly, I could see my right leg twist itself into the correct position. I was stunned. I could not fathom what I was seeing. My leg was moving itself into its rightful position in its socket. Shortly thereafter, the same happened with my left leg. I couldn't understand what was happening and then, like a flash of lightning, I remembered my last moment of life, was being pushed off a cliff. After that I blacked out. How is this possible? How am I alive? How are my legs able to put themselves back into place? This was shocking beyond reprieve. I could feel my heart beating faster and faster and I would only briefly catch my breath until I began screaming some more. I just stared at my legs in disbelief. I was in awe of my own body. It was one thing to be punched but to survive a fall and still be breathing is astounding to say the least. How could this be? How did I get here? Why am I inside a dilapidated motel? I looked to my right and on the dresser, there was a glass of water. I drank it and swung my legs to the side of the bed letting them hang freely. Once I calmed down and released my final scream, I slowly stood up. It was difficult. I had to steady myself very carefully. Once upright, I cursed and then quickly sat back on the bed. My legs were still healing. They had only just begun to repair themselves. I decided to rest some more. I looked at my arms and my thighs and my stomach and I was covered in bruises and dried blood. Yet again, like magic, one by one, I could see each bruise fade away. What was happening to me? How am I able to do this? Unless…since I could generate a forcefield with my mind, then maybe it was possible I could heal myself as well. But I was only discovering my powers. Healing requires the unlimited skill and concentration. Healing is never an easy feat. You must give into yourself completely; totally. I think I should rest still. I will try to calm myself and sleep my pain away, for now.

****

When I re-entered the motel, I was careful not to damage the front door lest I raise suspicion among the motel staff. She was still sleeping in her room. Her legs, it appeared were on the mend. I was happy to see the change in her. She was so beautiful when she slept. I wanted to kiss her forehead but I left her to her slumber.

"Wait…don't leave me," she said. "Who are you? What is going on? How did I heal so quickly?

"I healed you," I responded.

"You did. Thank you. But…who are you?"

"Marianne, it's me. It's Reagan or Esuahway whichever name you prefer is fine by me." I waited for her to respond in anger like she always has. I knew she hated me still for kidnapping her.

"You…Esuahway…you rescued me?!"

"Well, I wouldn't say that. I tried to get back to you in time to prevent your demise but I was too late. I'm always too late. I gave you some of my blood so you would heal faster."

"Wait…I don't understand. How does your blood heal…"

"Please Marianne. There is something about yourself you need to understand, you aren't quite human."

"What?"

"After you heal, I will tell you the truth."

"You can tell me now Reagan. I promise I won't get angry. I will hear you out."

"You are Nebuelah. You just don't remember. The reason is because your memory comes and goes. I've known about this for years. You are as old as I am. But the truth about your past has been concealed from you. I've watched you for so many years and for so many years you have slipped from me. I've seen you assume many identities, over and over and over again. Every time, I tried reaching out to you, I tried to ensnare you with romance, I tried relocating to various jobs to get close to you, I even tried enrolling in your university, I would follow you to the ends of the earth, no matter where you went or how far. I was always watching you in the shadows, always lurking and always longing."

"You were always watching me," she replied.

"Yes. Are you upset with me?"

"To be honest with you, I can't feel upset about anything. I am just trying to make sense of this all. My body aches still. I…this is too much for me…"

Marianne began crying and I went to her to hold her in my arms but I was worried she would rebuke my advances.

"Reagan, I mean, Esuah…I don't quite feel alright. My legs are twitching."

"It's alright Marianne. You are still healing. It should take another day or two for you to be completed healed. You needn't worry about anything I've said. Just rest."

"Oooooooooooh, my back hurts. My head aches. My stomach is nauseous. My legs feel like worms and I have no control over them."

"My blood is still coursing through your veins. Your body is repairing itself. It's like dying and being reborn all at once."

"Reagan, I mean, Esuahway, can you please hold me?"

"Yes. Of course, I can."

"Don't let me go. I feel so unwell right now."

"I promise I won't let you go. You can rest in my arms knowing all will be alright."

"Esuahway, how many times have I done this? Assumed different identities? Let you slip from me? I don't even know who or what I am? Why must I go through this so often? What have I done to earn this plight?"

"You were everything she desired. Nothing more and nothing less. You were her target pure and simple."

"Whose target?"

“The vampiress that I believe still lurks among us. She has tethered herself to you and controls your memory. This much I believe. She has somehow managed to link herself to you for centuries. If we joined forces, we could annihilate her. By forcing you to relive many lifetimes over, making you believe you are a mere mortal, she has controlled not only your fate but my own. I thought I killed her but apparently, I was wrong.”

“This evil demonic woman. Will she never leave you alone?”

“I think not. She seeks revenge because my attempt to end her life failed and she seeks revenge because the love I have for you is greater than anything I could ever hold dear. There is no measure to how much I care for you and she hates this. She wants not only to distort this but to corrupt it, pollute it and tarnish it. She takes pleasure in toying with you because she knows it is a blight on my life. She especially delights in watching you move clumsily about for so many centuries, not ever knowing your true identity or coming to terms with the full potential of your power.”

“Esuahway.”

“Yes.”

“I…I…I…”

Marianne collapsed onto the floor.

“Wake up Marianne. WAKE UP!”

She wasn’t responding. I put her in bed and held onto her and whispered sweet nothings in her ear. I kept talking to her, hoping that a part of her would awaken. I had seen this many a time. She would slip in and out of consciousness when confronted with the truth about her identity. If she continues this way, not knowing who she really is, floating from one persona to another, she would then black out and lose her memory for a long time and like a child, she would venture out into the world, under the prism of a child-like innocence that would endanger her life and mine as well. For she is tethered not only to the Elder vampiress but to me as well. I have always felt her pain no matter where she was, in this great big world. I have always felt her demise, her struggles, her happiness and even her confusion. She is my divine half and I am hers. I will never be at my fullest so long as she is not. Slowly, very slowly, her pinky finger gripped onto my ring finger. She wasn't totally lost to me and that was the greatest relief I could feel in that moment.

"Rea…gan…who…what…are…we…where…am…I"

"Shh," I whispered. "Just sleep. All will be well and you will remember your true self. Waking up from a false reality is never easy but embracing who you will be, when the time is right, will be. You are mine now forever Nebuelah and no one will ever take you from me ever again. Sleep and be still."

She gripped onto my hand even tighter. Her head fell onto my shoulder and her body, finally, slumped onto my chest. She recoiled for a bit and then nestled into my arm. I made sure to protect her head, especially. The trauma this woman has been through is much too much to bear and worst of all, having to witness it so many times over, was even worse for me knowing not how and when to intervene, always just watching over her like an angel. I felt strange and somewhat giddy. I feel after all this time, I will finally conquer the demon that hunts me still and poisons my dreams. This time, I will fight to the very end. I will conquer my demons both literal and figurative and Marianne will be restored. There will be no more delays, no more obstacles, no more mishaps and no more falsities. If we've been through all of this, I thought to myself, and still we are surviving, then it could not all have been in vain. There is a reason for all of this and Marianne – my Nebuelah – will help me secure this. She is stronger than she knows. She is more beautiful and more cunning than she knows. For if she is the reason, the vampiress has tormented me all these years, then she is clearly the key to her demise as well. She could have killed her anytime she pleased but she did not. She needs her like a babe needs milk to sustain itself. There is something more to this; something I am not seeing clearly. What is it that I am not seeing?

****

In my dream, I am holding a rosary and falling but this time, not to my demise. I falling into the arms of another. He is strong and he desires me. He defies his people. He defies his king. He defies even his family. He pleads with me to stay with him. I can't look away from him. He holds a key of some sort in his hands. He shows me this key and it is the very same rosary I was holding only it has transformed, before my eyes, into a crystal of some kind. It moves of its own free will. It has a mind of its own. It holds within it great secrets. I can feel my heart racing and sweat is pouring all over me. Blood begins to drain from every orifice on my body. She is standing not too far from me. In fact, she is standing directly behind me. A woman with shriveled hair and a look of distress about her face. She wears rags and points directly at the man. I stand to the side, drenched in my own blood, not understanding for the life of me what is going on. The man looks at me and grabs the crystal from my hand and pushes me aside. He lunges for the demonic woman and a battle ensues. The two are wrestling. They strike one another with such ferocity. They bare their fangs and their eyes glimmer. It was surreal: the way they fought, the way they leapt in the air, the way they sought to dominate the other. After many attempts at striking the woman demon, the man finally took the crystal and plunged it into her chest, twisting it with such force that it made a hole so large, he easily pulled out her heart and crushed it in front of her. I stood watching the entire scenario play out like a movie theatre goer. The man finally having struck the woman down, turned and looked at me and gave a sigh of relief. "It's over," he says to me. I just stare at him in disbelief. "Now, you must take the essence of that woman into your core." I stood still just looking at him. What on earth was he talking about? "You don't understand, do you? We can't allow her to come back. She can come back in a more hideous form and destroy worlds like she had destroyed yours and mine." Again, I stood still not saying a word, not moving a limb and just looked at the man; looked deeply into his eyes. His eyes were mesmerizing and hypnotic. "Stop wasting time Nebuelah. You know what you have to do. Do it quickly before your memory deceives you and leaves you once more!" I leaned forward, barely touching his forehead, and saw in his hand he held still the crystal. I grabbed it from him and cupped it in both of my hands. I looked at him once more and said: "this is what you've always wanted, isn't it?" I took the crystal and crushed it in my hands. I had forgotten all this time the strength I possessed. It was elating and erotic all at once, destroying this crystal. That's when the demonic woman, screamed and released a banshee cry that would shatter ordinary human ears but for he and I, nothing happened. She wasn't just dying, she was convulsing, deteriorating, shattering into pieces. Like the crystal, she was broken into pieces and each piece was set aflame and evaporated until only her head was left. She was screaming as every part of her body became fragmented. The harder I crushed the crystal, the more pain she felt. She was not dying an ordinary death. It was as though the many lives she had stolen from others was falling piece by piece; limb from limb; particle by particle. The man and I stood together, staring at her demise and relishing every moment of it. When she finally dissipated, so too was the crystal in my hand. Without rhyme or reason, the crystal or rather the fragments of it, mere sand on the ground, was now a rosary. The blood that was draining from every part of my body now receded and I was myself again. I was no longer perspiring. I remembered now who I was. I was Nebuelah, lover of Esuahway but most importantly, I was a witch. I could command the stars to sway, I could ask the moon to sing, and make the sun shine whilst the rain come out to play. I was the conjurer of all things in the natural world. I was sought by the king for my powers and my beauty. He wanted to have me to himself to gain an advantage over his enemies. Esuahway was not the vampiress' target, I was. She wanted to be both witch and vampire and her means of achieving that goal was through me. The rosary encapsulated the power she sought. The power I had accumulated, as a witch, and enveloped in a single jewel. The power to wield nature as I saw fit in one tiny object. Only now, as I looked down, at my hand, it wasn't a rosary I held, it was a necklace made of precious gems. I wore it round my neck to both embody and subdue the power within me. It was the key to my core. The vampiress knew this and stole it from me and through that object tethered herself to my identity. Without it, I would be lost and without memory and my power would be greatly diminished. This is why my life has been a never-ending cycle of hardship. When she attacked me in Esuahway's home, she gave me some of her blood. It was just enough to revivify my corpse. I was neither living nor dead. I was something…else.

****

"Marianne." I heard Esuahway's voice now. I must go to him. I must tell him of my newfound revelations. I can sense evil heading in our direction. Fully regenerated, I walked to the bathroom and washed my face. My legs are fully healed and so too is my neck. My back, my limbs and my stomach are restored and though I am not fully myself yet, I can feel myself elevating for the better.

"Marianne, I have brought you a meal to satiate your hunger."

"There's no time for that Reagan. I remember everything. I remember the token; my necklace. That is the way we defeat the vampiress. She is headed in our direction and we must confront her. That is how we get back our lives!"

TWENTY

THE CALLING

Esuahway was sitting by the window. He was staring at the outside world for hours on end. I would re-enter the room every so often to gather my clothes. I would make the bed, push back the curtains, eat the meal he had left for me and always he sat silent simply gazing out the window. I would, every so often, stare at him and wonder what he was thinking. How long has this man been running after me? How long had he been yearning for me? I wanted to tell him everything would be alright, at long last.

"Esuahway," I said. "I have eaten the meal you've left for me. I have tended to my belongings. We are ready to depart. Why do you continue to gaze out of the window so? Is everything alright?"

"I am overcome with fear and hope. I have been waiting for this moment for so long and now that it's here, I fear I may lose you all over again. Is this finally the end of our ongoing struggle? I have come close so many times only to falter again and again. I hope for change but I fear the worst."

"Esuahway, that push off the cliff awakened me. I had to go through everything to bring me to this point. You can't lose hope now. Together, we can conquer anything. I remember now who I am. I am a great witch, and a vampire too, like yourself. I am a hybrid and with this knowledge, I can help you defeat everything that has ever stood in your way. You can trust in that."

Esuahway turned slowly to meet my gaze and had such profound sadness on his face that it broke my heart. He wanted to ask questions but then stopped himself. He wanted to weep, but there were no tears where there should have been. He wanted to fold but was too ashamed to do so. Most importantly, he wanted to be held but cradled himself instead. He wanted to be cared for. He was tired of being so strong. I could feel his thoughts. And I wanted to be there for him as he had been for me. I touched his shoulder and let my hand linger for a moment. I stroked his hair and felt every fiber between my fingers. I conveyed to him that I was here now and everything would soon fall into place.

"Marianne," he said.

"It's Nebuelah," I replied.

"Nebuelah, do you care for me as I do for you. Do you remember what we had?"

"I…feel only remnants of the love we shared, if I am being honest. Some of my memory has returned. More will come to me in due time. Do not be hasty. I have only just begun to see more clearly. The jewel that encapsulates my power that is tethered still to the vampiress is still being controlled by her. She has wielded it to control my memory. This is why I have assumed so many identities, time and time again. This you already know. I understand now why you kidnapped me. You were hoping to wake me to my full potential. You wanted out of your pain and you wanted out of this centuries-old battle. I did not know who or what I was then but I do now. I am here for you now. So long as we get the jewel, and I receive it into my core, we will finally be set free. You will have your long-awaited freedom. Think on it and never let that thought go. The harder you focus on it, the more it will come to pass. I am a witch. I know such things to be true. Your thoughts are things. Your mind is the greatest resource you could ever possess. Do you believe me?"

He grabbed hold of my hand and stood up towering above me. I smiled at him. I wanted to reassure him that this time *is* the right time. He looked at me with a sadness that permeated his entire being. "I suppose," he said. "This time everything will be different. What then after our trial? When we defeat the demon woman, what will become of us?"

"That has not yet been written, my precious!" I said solemnly. "Would you like me to predict our future?"

"No. I think I should like the future to reveal itself."

"Naturally," I laughed.

"Nebuelah, I am sorry I choked…"

"PLEASE Esuahway, forget about it. You wanted, then, for me to see in myself what you have always known. You were overcome with anger. You have held onto so much pain for so long and it had to come out. I care not to remember that. I know where your heart lies."

"I sometimes wonder why it took so long. Why did it take centuries for you to return to me?"

"Must you know this?" I replied. "As a witch, I can assure you that time is relative and subject to our perception of it. You can ask a million different questions in a million different ways and ponder all of life's alternative paths for many a day but this will not aid your life's journey nor illuminate your soul with divine wisdom or grace. Things unfold as they should because we choose not to progress inwardly but rather chain to external entities for self-identification and validation. Do you understand? Just as the demon woman tethers herself to my jewel for power, you have tethered yourself to me for sustenance externally, and for selfhood. Without me, you feel as though you are nothing and without my jewel, I feel I am always lacking. Had you looked inwardly, you would have seen that everything happens in stages including your view of yourself. When you reach a desired stage inwardly, you pull towards you that which you seek. It could be a person, place or thing, a creature, foe or friend. You are what you seek. You are what you need. You are what you feel. You are the key to all. Witches and warlocks have known this for eons. That is the essence and source of our power. That is how we manipulate the natural forces of this earth."

"If I had looked inwardly, as you stated, would I have drawn you toward me sooner?"

"Yes, very much so. But you could not have known this. You cannot blame yourself for what you do not know."

"Can you teach me this? Are witches permitted to teach such things?"

"Do you wish to know how?"

"Yes, but only if you feel I am worthy of such a teaching."

"Your heart betrays you, Esuahway. Your heart and mind must be open to receive such power. You are still very much overcome with despair. When you have purged yourself of your dejection, you may come to me then."

"I love you Nebuelah. Please know this."

"I have always known."

TWENTY-ONE

Rapture of Ecstasy

We left the motel as it had been when first we entered it. We were careful not to leave any trace of blood lest a human discover and study it and reach the conclusion that vampires are real and living among them. Esuahway had given me his blood and some of it had splattered on the linen and very carefully I had washed the linen to cleanly perfection and dolefully made the bed. We called for a taxi and headed back to Esuahway's compound, the very same home he had imprisoned me in when first he captured me. Much to our surprise, the building still stood. The blast from our first encounter with a cryptid had left one bedroom partially destroyed. Esuahway searched the entire grounds to see if any creature, human or not, was present and when all was clear, he let me follow him onto the grounds. I was apprehensive upon entering, for memories of my capture, had suddenly reemerged in my mind. I was not myself then and I had to remind myself of that. It was simply my subconscious purging itself of painful memories. I had to push through it.

"Is everything alright?" asked Esuahway.

"Yes."

"You aren't dismayed, are you? I mean, the recollection of your kidnapping."

"It is alright Esuahway. You did what you had to do. I see that now." I smiled at him reassuringly.

We headed to the upstairs level and in the master bedroom, Esuahway had a hidden room behind a wall, when touched at the right place in a certain sequence of movements, would turn 180 degrees and reveal a plethora of weaponry of all kinds. I was stunned. I was absolutely beside myself.

"You've had all this weaponry, all this time!" I exclaimed.

"Yes. I could not reveal that to you. I knew you had immense power and if your subconscious mind had awakened, you would have easily found out about my weapons. I feared you would use them against me. I know all too well what you are capable of."

"I never would have hurt you."

"I wasn't certain then what you would have done!"

"I never meant any offense. You did what you felt best. This I know."

"What weapons would you like Nebuelah?"

"Which ones do you think I should take?" I smirked.

"I think anything you touch would service you well."

I pointed at the dagger and the chakram and lastly the sword.

"I think I'll take those," I said.

"Very well," he replied.

"I need to change my clothes. Do you mind if I have a moment to myself."

"Why would I mind?"

"Alright then. I'll be right back."

I left the master bedroom and went downstairs to the level beneath. I remembered there was a closet of women's clothing in the very room I was kept in. I removed the clothes I had been wearing for the past week and showered quickly. I giggled to myself thinking how the simple things in life are the most rewarding. The things we take for granted like walking, showering, reading, pondering, slumbering, eating, dancing; all are things that are refreshingly gratifying for the soul. They are simple yet fulfilling tasks. The greatest moments of our lives whether joyful or traumatizing define our characters and redirect our wills but the simple things are what makes life what it is. It's those down-and-out moments where we recharge, we get to resurrect our old selves into new avatars. I dried myself thoroughly. The bathroom was across the bedroom and I figured I could easily walk to the other room and dress there. After all, the rooms were across one another. As I exited the bathroom, there stood Esuahway in the doorway. I was stark naked and he took it upon himself to just stare at me.

"Do you mind?" I asked.

Esuahway would have blushed but being an undead thing, he obviously could not unless he had just fed.

"You are blocking my path!" I stated firmly.

Again, he stood still and looked at me.

"You know my eyes are up here!" I pointed to my face.

He slowly looked up into my eyes.

"Do you have something to say?" I stammered.

"I…I wanted to tell you that I secured us a vehicle to leave this compound. The vampiress has joined forces with the cryptids. I penetrated her thoughts and I can sense she is on her way here with the creatures."

"Alright."

Esuahway was still looking at me. He looked me up and down.

"STOP THAT!" I shouted.

"I'm sorry. Forgive me. I wanted…"

"It doesn't matter what you wanted - I am NAKED!"

"Yes. You are. I want you Nebuelah. I want you here and now."

"Please, this is not the time," I moaned. "I need to put my clothes on. And close your mouth, you act as if you've never seen a naked woman before."

"You are…"

"Don't say it!" I yelled.

"Beautiful."

"Oh, for heaven's sake! You are weak when you are with me. I think it best we separate and lead the cryptids in one direction and the vampiress in another. We need to distract one to defeat the other."

"I want you Nebuelah!" he shouted.

"You can do with me as you wish after we defeat our enemies."

"Now, I want you!" he shouted again.

"STOP IT! You need to focus!"

"Let me have you and then I will focus."

"That actually doesn't make any sense. Besides, I'm a bit cold from the shower. I would prefer to be dressed."

Esuahway grabbed me from behind and started to kiss me on my neck, shoulders and down my back.

"What are you doing?" I slapped him across his face.

"Just a moment. Please."

"We need to get a move on. How can you think of physical pleasures at a moment like this?"

"When you are near me, that is all I think about."

"Oh, dear Lord!" I rolled my eyes. "If I let you have your way with me, for a brief moment, will you then focus and get ready for our departure?"

"Yes. Anything you wish, my love."

"Well," I paused. "I won't let you. Now, focus, please!"

He slipped a hand onto my breast and squeezed it ever so gently. I smacked his arm away and kicked him back slamming him into the wall.

"I'm starting to think you really only wanted me back in your life to satisfy your carnal pleasures. Typical."

"And what if I did?"

"You said you wanted to end your centuries battle with that demon of a woman!"

"I do but I don't see any harm in getting back to the one that loved me most in all the world! Can I not procure both?"

"Well, realistically, yes, you can but Esuahway, I don't feel the way you do. I don't know what idealized version of me you have in your mind and I still don't quite feel the same way you do. I don't harbor any hatred for you but I don't feel the elation you do when you are near."

"Then I am nothing to you?"

"No. You are very important to me. But can we not do one thing before we engage in the other?"

He sat still seemingly engaged in other matters of the mind.

"ALRIGHT!" I shouted. "Come here to me Esuahway."

He approached me without hesitation.

"Get down on your knees."

He obeyed.

"Ok. Let's see what we've got here." I grabbed hold of his face. "We've got a man who is love sick with the same woman for centuries. He is distracted by her beauty and her strength and wants to ravish her. He wants her body, mind and soul and he won't focus on the current dilemma because she is all he thinks about! Am I right so far?"

"Yes," he smiled.

"If we don't get hold of the precious jewel and destroy it by releasing its potency into my core, the vampiress will forever roam free, regenerating in many hideous forms, taking all, she desires without a care in the world, unless we put a stop to it. Am I still right so far?"

"Yes," he smiled again.

"Though, my memory has been partially restored, I still do not recall everything, like my connection to you. And while time is running out, I may very well lose what I have already regained. Am I still right so far?"

"Yes," he smiled again.

"The cryptids and the vampire woman demon are upon us and if we can sense they are near, they too, can sense our presence. Is this correct?" I asked.

"Yes," he replied again.

"If my dream can unlock the secret to all we hold dear and end this ongoing war, maybe then, upon conquering that aspect of our journey, my purpose in being with you shall be unlocked forevermore as well? Do you agree with this hypothesis?"

"Yes. It makes perfect sense to me," he said.

"Have you learned nothing from what I have said, my sweet? You must first work inwardly discovering your power from within to find the key to all you desire! One increment at a time – that is the way of nature. We will only grow stronger after our battle together and that is the key to learning more about our love. Maybe then, I will feel as you do and be one with you. Until then, we focus on the battle at hand."

"First," he said, "I must battle as one with you, to learn more about you, to re-discover my love for you."

"Precisely," I smiled. "By George I think he's got it!" I laughed and laughed until he joined me in my laughter.

"Now, shall we get ready for battle!" I demanded.

"Not until I kiss you," he said.

"Oh! For fuck's sake, you weren't listening! You were pretending to listen the entire time."

"Isn't that what men do best!"

"Bullocks! You've had centuries to learn better!"

He slipped his arm around my waist and pulled me closer to him. He slipped his hand down to my buttocks and pulled my legs up around his waist.

"Will you resist me?" he asked.

“Yes,” I replied. He was shocked! He wasn’t prepared for that response.

“I knew that would astonish you!” I tightened my legs around his waist and bent myself backwards pulling him down and over me. I flung him across the room and his massive build broke the cabinet dresser.

“Seriously Esuahway! Let’s get ready. We have all the time in the world for frolicking.”

TWENTY-TWO

BATTLE CRIES

We left the compound the following morning. I always forget that Esuahway is immune to the sun's rays. He is ancient beyond the calculations of any modern-day calendar. It seems, I too, am susceptible to the foolery of Hollywood films. Vampires are as complex as humans are and are as varied too. They do not set ablaze with the sun's rays but are merely weakened by it. Esuahway's power is limitless. He is as powerful during the day as he is during the night.

In order not to be tracked, Esuahway set his compound on fire burning everything to the ground. He did not want any cryptids of any kind, picking up our scent and knowing where we were and thus where we would be headed. Esuahway owned several properties, some in North America and a few in Europe and he had investments in various portfolios and offshore accounts. We could easily start anew in a new country if we chose to.

We headed back to the border of England and Scotland and westward toward the mountains where last we came upon the cryptids. It was surreal heading back to the very cliff, upon which, I was sentenced to death. I remember those last moments and the fear that encased my soul as I was falling.

"Does it hurt still?" asked Esuahway.

"No. I'm alright. I'm over it. If not for that fall, I would not have regained most of my memory."

Esuahway continued driving for another five hours. The scenic countryside was beautiful and I was excited at the wonder of it all. I would sometimes turn my gaze to Esuahway and look at the details of his face, his hands, his hair, his eyes especially were exceptionally fascinating. I loved the tint of his glassy eyes. My eyes were normal for all intents and purposes. The vampire half of me manifests only when I use my powers, otherwise, I appear as human.

I must have fallen asleep because I could feel Esuahway shake my shoulder abruptly all of a sudden.

"Have we arrived? Are we back at the cryptid compound?" I asked.

"Yes. Are you up for the challenge facing us?"

"Aren't I always?"

"Yes. You certainly are. Let us grab our weapons."

Esuahway opened the trunk of the car and gave me my weapons while he took his. We were careful not to make any sounds as we left behind our car and walked into the caves. We camped near the entrance anticipating the cryptids that would emerge near nightfall. However, right before the sun would set, we would set a trap for the hideous creatures.

"Do you think we will win this time?" asked Esuahway.

"We have to win. What choice do we have?" I replied. "Shh, I hear something. It's not too far from where we are. Listen for it."

With his heightened sense of hearing, Esuahway listened intentionally and concurred that he heard something as well. Whilst gathering our weapons, we moved locations with great immediacy. We headed in the opposite direction of our parked car which was at least 20 kilometers away. We moved stealthily. I was always five feet behind Esuahway and always ready with weapon in hand. We could feel the entity encroaching upon us and we decided to quicken our pace. It was then, as I was running, that I tripped a wire and was thrusted upside down with a cord around my right ankle. I was lifted 30 feet into the air and left dangling.

"Esuahway," I shouted. "It's a trap. Run. Save yourself."

He turned round and saw I was hanging from the trees and was about to leap into the air to grab hold of me but was suddenly thrust back by an invisible force.

"Why are you doing this Nebuelah?"

"It's not me!" I yelled.

"No. It wouldn't be, would it?" screeched a woman.

"Vampiress. Evil demon woman," shouted Esuahway.

Behind the woman, were a clan of dogmen ready and willing to battle. They were ravenous beings and would do anything their vile leader commanded!

"Finally, you appear my sweet!" proclaimed the vampiress.

"Yeah, to kick your ass!" I exclaimed.

"Haha! Such words you say," she replied haughtily. "Do you really think hanging upside down you are a match for me!"

"We'll see, won't we? Once I break loose!"

In that moment, I hoisted myself upward, bending at the waist, and with all my force, and quite the force I had, I pulled at the cord until the entire branch broke off. I fell to the ground but I was unfazed. I stood up and ran towards the vampiress and pushed her with all my might, she went flying backwards in the air and then slammed into a tree.

"Esuahway," I shouted. "Attack the cryptids!"

He grabbed his sword and swung at the creatures, one by one. He decapitated heads, slashed at guts and ripped apart limbs without so much as a blink of the eye. He was a one-man army and I was hellbent on destroying his archnemesis. I would have my token, the jewel. I would retrieve my necklace and I would regain my full memory and power once and for all.

"You cannot defeat me," cried the vampiress.

"We'll see about that! Now, give me what I want. You know what we've come for," I declared.

"You barely even remember me!"

"I remember you were ugly then and you're still ugly now!"

"Hahahahaha, you really think words will hurt me."

"No. But I do enjoy insulting you. Makes things a little more fun, don't you think?"

"Foolish woman!"

The vampiress lunged at me, leaping high in the air and then descending on my stomach. The pain was intense. I was strong enough to push her off and pin her to the ground.

"Give me back my jewel! No longer shall you wield it to control my mind. I want what is rightfully mine! If you disobey, I will kill you!"

"Try, with all your might, you insipid little witch, I will give over no such power to you!"

We struggled on the ground, wrestling with one another, trying desperately to dominate the other.

"Tell me, you bitch, how did you get it from me? How did you take that which is so precious to me!?"

"It was quite easy. When your foolish Esuahway cried over your decrepit body and mourned your waste of a death, I waited until the following day, after your burial, to dig up your corpse and take the token from your neck! You never told him! He never knew the full extent of the power you beheld and even now, he still doesn't know!"

Esuahway could hear every word of our conversation and he almost lost his concentration, whilst staving off the cryptids from attacking me.

"What is she talking about Nebuelah?" he asked.

"I don't know what this monstrous thing is talking about?"

"Oh, yes you do!" replied the vampiress.

"Shut up! You know damn well I know nothing. After all, you've been controlling my mind all this time. I was living one useless semblance of a mortal life after another, for centuries. That was all YOU!"

"Oh, but you've always known, in the back of your mind Nebuelah, you have always known."

"You are really starting to irritate me woman. Now, hand over the jewel or your head is mine!"

I gave her a blow to the head and neck. I wanted her destroyed. I wanted to feel her essence leave her body. I was not only going to take back my precious jewel but I would consume and then annihilate her soul too.

"Esuahway, are you sure you want to fight so hard for the love of your life. She isn't what she seems. Hahahahaha." The vampiress cackled and sneered. She hissed at me and made no qualms about exposing her fangs to me. She tried biting at me several times but I shoved and slapped her face until she could no longer bear the force of my strength.

"You can beat me all you want," the vampiress laughed. "But you will never get what you want!"

"Where is it? Where is the jewel?" I shouted.

"Well, it isn't with me. You can strangle me all you like you'll never get it."

"You are infuriating woman!" I wanted to rip her head off but she kicked me furiously in the ribs and I lost my breath for a few moments.

"Esuahway, help me!" I stammered.

"The jewel, my pretty, has never been with me. Yes, I stole it from you and I harnessed its power but that was centuries ago. I was never the one to control your thoughts or your mind."

"What nonsense do you speak of?" I cried.

"Why, your precious Esuahway, he was the one who was manipulating you this entire time! I'm surprised you hadn't noticed! He's had the jewel in his possession the entire time."

"Esuahway, what does she mean? Esuahway, where are you?" I looked all around me and could not see him anywhere. I looked back to face the vampiress and she too was gone! The cryptids had vanished too. I was all alone. It was like nothing had happened. I was exasperated. Everyone and everything had dissipated before my eyes and I had no recourse to move forward. I was made to start all over again. I would walk away, carrying only my weapons in hand and never look back. I was outcast once more. I was alone once more. I have always been alone.

TWENTY-THREE

REMAINS OF TRUTH

1021 A.D.

I was lost in the sea of my drowning thoughts. I received Nebuelah as the perfect being. When I first beheld her, I knew she was my destiny, my all and my everything. The last thing I would do is betray my true love and Nebuelah is my true love. She is the apple of my eye, the reason I wake up every day and sleep every night. She knows me like no other and I want her as she wants me. I would never take from her that which she treasured most. How could I tell her the truth? I need her precious jewel. I need the jewel she wears around her neck. I need it to save myself and my family from impending doom. If I could harness its power, I could use it to prevent the king from killing my family, for surely, he will discover my betrayal. I will create a shield that will encase my family's home from his soldier's attacks. The king will learn of my treachery soon enough; my love for Nebuelah and behead me for taking her in my arms every night. She is betrothed to the king and I stole what is rightfully his. My death cannot be avoided unless I use Nebuelah's power to gain my protection. If I return the jewel to her, before she realizes it was taken, she will be none the wiser. My family and I will not have to endure the king's wrath. He will fear me when he sees me wield the power of a divine priestess witch. I will only use the jewel's power for good. When the night falls, and Nebuelah returns once more to my arms, I will wait for her to fall asleep and borrow from her what I know she can do without. I wonder if she can sense my impending doom? Maybe if I asked her for help, she would aid me in my struggle? Why is it so hard for me to tell her how I feel? I want her to know I am everything she could ever want and trust and be all the man she'll ever need! Oh, Nebuelah, should we forget our love altogether? You go your way and fold into the king's world? And I find another like you but never quite like you? Are we risking the lives of our families to fulfill our carnal pleasures? Are we selfishly pursuing a dream that will never come to pass? Should we remain lovers in our fantasies and dreams? Or should we fulfill our highest calling and build a life that beams? Should I ask you to stay with me or should I ask you to go? My heart forever tells me that I should ask of you no more. When the day becomes the night, I come alive looking in your eyes. Tell me Nebuelah, what shall I do? Forget your love and forget this plight? When next she falls, to me, I trust her soul to keep. When next we make love, I will tell her sweet nothings and fold into her like she adores. I will ask for an exhibition of her power and accept her for all she is. The time is nearing and soon we will meet again. Soon Nebuelah will be as one with me and I will relish in her desires, in her flesh, the very scent of her hair. She will forge a bond with me forever unbreakable and she will yearn for nothing more than the love we've formed and make sacred our bond in the name of her power evermore.

"Nebuelah, my love. Will you show me your true self? Will you let me in your world and show me your great power so that I may better understand you?"

"Yes, Esuahway, I will show you all of me and together, we shall be as one."

"Let me in and I'm yours. Let me show you how much I love you."

"That you shall do for me and so much more."

I grabbed hold of Nebuelah and gave her everything her heart desired. After we consummated our union, she let me hold the jewel in my hands. It was, by far, the most beautiful jewel I had ever beheld. It shimmered and shone brighter than any star I had ever seen in the sky, and always brighter than the glimmer of my Nebuelah's eyes.

"Look Esuahway. The jewel reciprocates your love. It knows you better than you know yourself. With it, you can manipulate the forces of nature, command the animals in the forests, and create any force you desire to protect the ones you love but should your heart be corrupted, the power you wield could destroy worlds and consume your soul, feasting upon it for all time."

"May I use it? To protect us Nebuelah? Should the king find out about..."

"Hush Esuahway. I will see to it that the king knows nothing of our consort. I will ensure our love exists now and forever. You need not worry for I will look after you and I shall be your protector."

"But you don't understand Nebuelah! The king is very powerful. I have been his steward for many years. He is not one to be toyed with. He will not be betrayed nor dismayed. He is the most ruthless of rulers our people have ever seen! Nebuelah, I respect your great power but you don't understand what you say when you say you will protect us both. The king's temper is unmatched. He will not suffer fools!"

"Please Esuahway. Do not worry yourself. You give away much of your true nature and vibrant essence when you worry foolishly."

"No. Nebuelah, I concur not with you. I shall have your jewel and I shall do well to wield it to our benefit."

I tore the jewel from her neck and ran from her as fast as I could. Nebuelah chased after me and told me to stop but I wouldn't listen. I was determined to prove my strength to her. I concentrated with all my might and focused my energy onto the jewel. I held it tightly in my grasp and asked for protection for myself, for Nebuelah and my family. I asked for it to answer my prayer and to demand the king release Nebuelah and give her to me. I wanted a savior to answer my prayer, affirm my desires and release my fears. And the jewel obeyed. It did more than placate my requests, it brought forth a woman of great strength. It brought forth a mighty vampiress.

"You called. I answered. I will do as you command if you do as I wish."

"Yes. Of course. I shall do anything you ask. You are the manifestation of the jewel's power, are you not?"

"Why, yes of course, I am. My name is Nephthys. I will remove the king, your primary obstacle and protect your family from his wrath. You shall have your Nebuelah and keep her for eternity. All this you shall have in exchange for one simple thing."

"Yes, what is it?"

"I want your soul. I want your blood."

"As you wish, Nephthys."

TWENTY-FOUR

DISTANCE RECLAIMED

"You thought you could have it all, didn't you?" said Nephthys.

"I know I can. I won't let you stand in my way this time," I replied.

"Oh silly boy, silly Esuahway. You only know half the story. You really think a person as selfish as you can have it all. The reason you are in this mess is because you always put yourself first. It's always Nebuelah this or Nebuelah that. It's always – protect my family like this or destroy the king like that! It's always been about you and your needs, hasn't it?" asked Nephthys.

"You wanted Nebuelah from the moment you saw her and you hated the king because he denied you her flesh. You are as corrupt as he is. You wanted Nebuelah's power for yourself as well. Just as he did. You and he are exactly alike!"

"THAT'S NOT TRUE! I loved Nebuelah and I still love her. The king would have used her. I wanted to revere her!"

"You've trapped us both in an alternate dimension, you fool! You have no idea what you are doing with the jewel, do you? You could never understand its power because your heart is black. Nebuelah warned you, didn't she? But instead, the arrogant being that you are took matters into your own hands! Silly, silly, boy. Always a child! Hahahahahaha!"

Enraged, I ran toward Nephthys and shoved her to the ground. I pummeled her with my fists. This did not deter her. She, in turn, kicked me and sent me flying backwards. Two elder vampires fighting, with powers of equal measure, could spend eternity battling each other with no end in sight. I grabbed her throat and began choking her. I wanted to see the life drain from her eyes. She was not the demonstration of the jewel's essence I had wished for. She stalked me for days on end and waited for the opportune moment to appear before me, pretending to be the physical manifestation of jewel's power. I was surprised once I came into full understanding of what was happening. Nebuelah was right. If your heart is corrupt or your desires and motivations are purely selfish, you will attract exactly that into your life. Nephthys was exactly that. I must find a way to will myself back to Nebuelah, back to our time. I cannot stand this realm let alone fight Nephyths for all time.

"You can't find your way back, can you Esuahway? It looks like it's just you and me together forever in this place."

"Be silent woman!" I shouted.

We fought and we fought. I wasn't going to let this *thing* control me forever. Yes, I wanted the jewel for myself and yes, I was selfish in my motivations but my love for Nebuelah was real and the essence of that could never be removed from my heart. That's it – isn't it? I have to remember why I did what I did in the first place and why I disobeyed Nebuelah and stole her jewel. I wanted to show her that I could place her needs above my own and that she was my everything. That's the key. That's how I get back home. I must concentrate with all my might. I won't battle this fiend any longer. I bring the battle back to Nebuelah. I bring the battle back home.

****

I was walking the trail Esuahway and I had walked on when heading toward the caves. There was no reason to stay on these grounds. Like magic, the fight had disappeared before my eyes. I walked as slowly as I possibly could. I wasn't keen on returning back to his compound nor was I interested in moving forward with life. I needed resolution. I wanted to regain my full memory and fully become who I was meant to be. How long have I walked this earth? How long have I been *alive*? I pondered upon such things as I headed back to the car. I would let the sound of the leaves, crushed under my feet, put me into a trance. I was enamored by the sound and I let it drown into the depth of my body.

Suddenly, a flash of light flickered behind me. I could feel it shake the ground. I turned around to see what it was and falling from the sky, I could see the vampiress and Esuahway enveloped in an orb. I was dazed. I almost stumbled turning round the other way. My feet buckled beneath my knees. I began running towards them. They were fighting still and thrusting fists of such fury.

"Esuahway," I yelled out. He turned toward me and stared in my direction but then quickly looked away.

"Esuahway," I cried out again. I ran toward him. The intensity of the forcefield blew me away and I stumbled backwards yet again. They were engrossed in battle still and I was all too ready to join them. I remembered that the jewel was still in their possession. I needed to retrieve it and take it into my core. Once I shook off my initial shock, I ran full blast towards the dueling vampires and generated a forcefield powerful enough to debilitate the existing forcefield encircling them. I broke down that barrier and delivered a kick so powerful I forced the vampiress to fall backwards. I jumped in the air and landed with both feet on her chest.

"Give me my jewel demon!"

"The name is Nephthys, Nebuelah and I don't have your precious jewel. It's your beloved Esuahway who has been wielding it the entire time!"

I kept my foot on Nephthys' neck and turned to Esuahway.

"What is she talking about?"

"I stole the jewel from you Nebuelah, centuries ago. I wanted to use the power of it as I saw fit but only to protect us, my family and destroy the king so he could never take you from me. You were mine, Nebuelah! Mine!"

"I don't remember this."

"You came to me, one night, as you always do and I waited for an opportune time to grab the jewel from your neck. I beckoned it to give me ultimate power and instead it brought Nephyths to me!"

"He is the reason your memory fades in and out. He had the jewel the entire time and blamed me for it!" shouted Nephthys.

"Esuahway, give it to me! NOW!" I proclaimed.

"I'm sorry Nebuelah. I thought I could handle its force. I only wanted you to stay with me."

"Esuahway, I said give it to me now!" I professed once more.

"Nebuelah, please don't hurt me," he cried.

"I will do more than that if you don't hand it over to me now!"

Still holding my foot on Nephthys' neck, I forced Esuahway to march forward, toward me, using my powers. I forced open his hands and there it was – the source of my power – I beckoned it to come to me. It floated in the air and hovered before me. I grabbed hold of it with my left hand and crushed it. I took its remnants and swallowed it. I let every grain permeate my veins and enter my blood stream. I was elated to feel its essence, its power inside of me. My eyes could see things for what they really were. It was as though the trees, the birds, the waters, everything had a spirit and a life force of its own. I could see all of nature breathe.

"Nephthys," I said. "Your time has come to an end. You shall live no more. You have waged enough wars, tearing down nation after nation to satiate your blood lust. You destroyed Esuahway's kingdom. You played upon his desires for power and his love for me and for that you shall exist no more. I bind you Nephthys. I bind you to do no harm and to dissipate into nothingness."

My words manifested a power unlike any other power I possessed. With my thoughts, I could create anything from nothing and what I sought for most in that moment was Nephthys' destruction. I used all my mind to focus a power so great that Nephthys' body began to burn. One limb, after the other, starting first with her feet and working its way up to her head, she was set ablaze. Like a banshee, she screamed a wail so loud and so grating that the earth shook. She was turning to ash before my eyes. Her ashes were rising into the air until finally, she was no more and at last I was rid of the demon Nephthys.

I regained my memory. I remembered my past. I remembered Esuahway and the private moments we shared. I remembered his blind devotion for me. I turned round and looked at him. He was kneeling on the ground with his head in his hands. I think he was weeping. I stared in his direction for quite some time. His whole existence was defined by me and he was the one who was lost the entire time. I was merely slumbering inside lesser versions of myself. I wanted to leave Esuahway there. He needs time to heal. He needs to process what he has done. I began walking away. I left him there to his devices and I didn't look back.

"Nebuelah," he cried. "Are you leaving me again? I never meant for things to get this out of hand? Please come back."

I kept walking. I heard him – yes, but he needs to grieve. I cannot continue to allow him to depend solely upon me for his sustenance. He must find meaning outside of his love for me. I thought this best and if the universe should decree that we must, once more, be united, then so shall it be. I wanted to hold him and tell him everything will be alright but I wouldn't want him to fold into me and lean into me, knowing only me as his source of strength. His love is beautiful. I admire this greatly but he needs time away from me to truly comprehend the greatness that is ***his*** power. His power lies in his identity. And his identity is a great one. If only he could see that for himself. "I love you Esuahway. I truly do," I whispered to myself. "It is time we let each other go and forge new paths with our resurrected selves."

TWENTY-FIVE

ESUAHWAY'S LONGING

She left me stranded by the caves. She left the weapons I had given her too. She walked away and didn't look back. I was mortified by everything I'd been through only to find Nebuelah did not return the love I felt for her. I was nothing to her. She just let me go.

To say I was beside myself in that moment was an underestimation. I truly thought I was fighting for something worthwhile. In the end, Nebuelah only became more so herself. I was but a fraction of her story but she was writing that story the entire time. I gathered the weapons and walked drearily back to the car. I drove for miles in no particular direction. I kept thinking Nebuelah would appear before my eyes but clearly, she made her choice. I truly believed if she regained her full memory, she would remember how much we meant to each other, after all these centuries. I miscalculated horribly. Perhaps, it is best. Perhaps, letting her go means I can finally create, for myself, a new identity and life that, subconsciously, I have always desired and wanted. I must see what this new world offers. I must see its wonders, its glories, its hopes and dreams. There is so much I haven't explored.

"Nebuelah," I spoke aloud. "Wherever you are, I hope you are doing well and I hope you have forgiven me for all my trespasses. I never meant to bring so much destruction into your life. I really truly wanted you to be with me eternally. Can you hear me?"

I continued driving for many hours on end, just driving and not caring where I went. I wanted to forget my beautiful Nebuelah. She had moved on so easily without a care in the world. I was beside myself thinking she would return to me once her power was returned to her but instead, she forged ahead, creating a new rhyme and reason for being.

I decided to head to Canada. I had another compound located there and I would settle on the East Coast, getting my bearings first in a motel. It would be a serene place to take my mind off things and forget about the past days' events. I would spend time among mortals and rest in the security that they knew not what I was. I would learn of their ways and speak with them as I had centuries ago when I hid amongst them.

Finally, after driving for so long, I headed to the airport and purchased a one-way ticket to Canada. I would board that plane and never look back.

****

"Hi. My name is Joan. How are you?" A woman spoke. She looked at me with the most serene eyes. I hesitated for a moment and tried to gather myself. I am still, often times, struck by the forwardness of women these days. They do not necessarily wait for men to take charge and this is both exhilarating and foreign to me.

"Hello," I responded.

"Are you new to Canada? You don't look like any of the locals?"

"Yes. I am."

"Cool." She stood completely still and gazed at me for a long moment. "Do you plan on staying in Canada?"

"Yes, I suppose."

"Let me show you around town! I'd love to do it if you don't mind, of course. Are you familiar with all the hangouts? Have you made any friends?"

"No, I suppose I haven't."

"Well, like I said, my name is Joan and I'll be your friend."

"I'd like that," I said. "I'd like that very much."

The following evening, Joan and I met at Durty Nelly's Irish Pub and Joan was gracious enough to tell me about the local bands that perform in Nova Scotia. She introduced me to the bartender and her group of friends. Altogether, they were Jack, Marcus and Stella.

"This is…I forgot to ask your name! What is your name?"

"My name is Reagan."

"Alrighty then. Jack, Marcus, Stella, let me introduce you to Reagan. We met a few days ago and he is new to Nova Scotia."

"Hello everyone," I said.

"Hi Reagan," replied Marcus, followed by Jack and Stella. "Can you sing?"

"No. I suppose I can't."

"Then you're in for a treat. I do. I'm going up on stage next."

"Best of luck Marcus," I smiled.

Marcus joined his bandmates on the stage and they played through a set of songs of the rock genre. The entire time I could feel Joan's gaze upon me. She would not deviate her stare to the left or right of her. She would remain intent on keeping her focus on me. To say that it disturbed me was a trivialization. I would every so often, turn and look at her but I would, for the most part, not show any fear and simply ignore her. I could sense something was not quite right with her but I let things be. I was always on guard even when I appeared not to be. I would venture into the mortal world every so often to learn of the post-modern customs practiced among humans today but that did not mean I was not wary of humans either. In packs, humans can do much damage to vampires. I had to be cautious in all my dealings whether with humans or non-humans.

I was on guard with Joan. I would not reveal that which she needn't know.

"Joan!" shouted Marcus from the stage. "Why don't you come up here and give the audience a demonstration of your voice."

"At last," I thought to myself. This woman would busy herself with something constructive other than gawking at me. She joined her bandmates on stage and belted a tune or two. I used this opportunity to excuse myself from the premises. I said my goodbyes to Stella and Jack and told them I would reconvene at a later date as I had tasks to tend to. I believe it was Stella who pleaded with me to stay but I reassured her that I would join them again, some other time.

As I exited the bar, I could feel someone was lurking close behind me. My senses were keen and highly sensitive, heightened, as one would call it, being immortal for so long it comes naturally. I began walking back to the apartment I had rented for a few days. I would not be staying in that residence for too long as I often find moving from place to place to be safest. But, as I was walking, I could hear feet shuffling on the grass but a stone's throw away from me. I would turn behind me and find no one, nothing there. Once again, I showed no fear. I moved ever so quickly and called out to a taxi. I decided rather than head straight home, I would ask the driver to show me round the most popular tourist destinations. I was in no mood to be followed back home and whatever or whoever was lurking behind the shadows would not be interested in Nova Scotia's "hot spots".

Suffice it to say, I actually did enjoy my time travelling from one location to another. By the time, I had asked the driver to send me to my destination, three hours had passed. When I entered my apartment, everything was as it was. I had but a desk, a chair, a bed and a mini-fridge. I laid myself on the mattress and turned on the TV. I did not watch anything in particular, I just let the TV run. I barricaded the door and kept all the windows shut. In just one more hour, the sun would rise and I would slumber. While I don't have to rest during the daylight hours, I feel it rejuvenates me and it is nice to just close my eyes. I would often dream of Nebuelah and sometimes I would dream of nothing at all. Every now and then, I imagined what she must be doing or where she must be going or whom she is talking to. She could dazzle anyone in conversation. She was especially very good at mesmerizing humans. I was in awe of her always. I could do the very same but nowhere near her capacity, especially when she chose to control others. And I often times, chose not to wield my power over humans unless absolutely necessary.

I decided finally it was time to sleep. I let myself fall on the mattress and shut my eyes until nightfall. And once again, I imagined myself being consoled by Nebuelah. I longed for her still and I remembered the days, centuries ago, when she would wait for me to fall asleep in her arms.

TWENTY-SIX

JOAN AND THE GANG

"Did you get a good feel for him?" asked Marcus.

"Yeah, I certainly did," replied Joan.

"Do you think we should follow him?"

"No. Not quite yet. If we do that, he will know something is up. We want to make sure he is comfortable where he is and suspects nothing."

"You're right," replied Jack.

"Of course, I'm right. I'm always right," stated Joan matter-of-factly.

"When should we strike at him?" asked Jack.

"I haven't the slightest clue. He isn't with that partner of his. That woman that he's always around. At least, in my visions, there is always a woman around him. I can barely make out her face though."

"Is she shrouding herself, in your visions? And what about the police. I thought you feigned your death to lead them on a wild goose chase?" asked Stella.

"Yes. I did feign my death. It most definitely distracted the police. They have no clue what is really going on. Once my body was placed in a morgue, I used my strength to escape my confines. As for Nebuelah shrouding herself...hmmm...can that be done? I mean, can a person shroud themselves in another's vision?"

"Well, you said she's a witch with vampiric blood. I take it she can do so much more than we could ever imagine."

"Yes. She could be intentionally shrouding her face in my visions. She may very well be aware that we are trying to snuff her out."

"Does she know where we are located?" asked Stella.

"I think she can sense us trying to sense her."

"Joan," said Stella, "are you sure about this? Are you sure we are to go up against this woman witch! What if this means the death of us all?"

"She can't do anything. As far as I know, she hasn't regained her full power yet and she hasn't her full memory of her past and who and what she used to be. She probably still thinks I'm her friend from England. But Reagan, who was watching her the entire time we were watching him, he always stands in the way! I can't stand him. Little does he know, I kept tabs on him the entire time. I tracked him down in England but didn't enter his compound because I wasn't sure on how to take him down and I saw Marianne was with him. Until she escaped his grasp, I couldn't really do much. But somehow, while I was following them around, I lost track of them. And there was another; an elder vampiress. There was some great battle of some sort and then suddenly, they all just vanished into the air. I slumbered for many days, having to bury myself in the ground. I had no choice and just waited. Until finally, one day I saw Reagan appear out of nowhere and drive off in a car. I then followed him to Canada."

"When they all disappeared," asked Jack, "do you know where they went?"

"You see, that's what I can't figure out. I don't get how people just dissolve into the air. Even with our powers, that can't be done. You don't just de-materialize...unless."

"Unless what?" inquired Stella.

"Unless there is more to this than I had anticipated. Maybe they possess even greater power than I had realized."

"Well, now that he's here, in Canada and Marianne seems to be nowhere in sight, how should we proceed next?" demanded Marcus.

"I think we should just keep a watch on Reagan for the moment. I think I know what motel he currently resides but he makes it damned near impossible to get into the front door. He is aware he is being watched. He is always cautious. He is never predictable either. I lost track of him when he left the bar yesterday."

"Joan, are you sure we should go through with this?" asked Stella.

"You have doubts?"

"Well, no, I just...well, I'm afraid of Marianne. She is formidable. She is unmatched. She can destroy an entire village is she chose to. I would not want to incur her wrath."

"Stella, you better not be backing out on me now. I let you and Jack join our coven so we could be that much more powerful against those two! Marianne has somehow vanished into some other dimension. Who cares!? The point is she isn't here. Once we take down Reagan, and take into us his blood, our power will grow a hundredfold and we will reap the benefits of this reward!"

"The cryptids tried to waste his ass," said Marcus. "But they didn't succeed."

"Yeah, that's why we have to step in."

"Hey Joan, what about the vampiress?"

"What about her?"

"Did she perish in the great battle?"

"Well, as far as I know she did."

"And there is no way of getting her back."

"Maybe. I am still working out the details. I would have loved to have gotten my hands on her power too."

"Do you think Reagan knows what is going on? I mean, does he fully comprehend what is headed his way?"

"I'm not too sure. He seems lost at times. It's like without that Marianne chick, he is only a shadow of his former glory. At first, I thought it was his love for her but there is something amiss."

"I hope you're right about all this," Stella states.

"Of course, I'm right! Do you doubt me?"

"No, Joan. I don't. I just..."

"You just what?"

"If Reagan killed the vampiress. What then could he do to us?"

"You see, that's just it. I don't think it was he who killed her."

"What do you mean?" asked Jack.

"There was a lot going on during the great battle and I could not make out everything that was happening as I had to hide miles away during the fight but Marianne may have done the killing. I'm not entirely sure it was Reagan."

"So, the plan is…what exactly?" asked Stella.

"The plan," I answered, "is to destroy Reagan, take his essence into ourselves, make sure no one gets in our way and fulfill the vampiress' wish to return to our realm. The dogmen were unsuccessful in fulfilling her desire and so we shall take their place."

"But I thought you said the vampiress was killed!"

"She was but she can return!"

"How is this possible?"

"Reagan has the core inside him as well. I speculate he must. That is why he survived the great battle and although Marianne did not, Reagan has the other half of the token within him. He could be feigning his possession of the sacred token or he is truly unaware it's in his grasp. If he is unaware then all the better for us! We can easily subdue him and get what we need. With this core, we can travel back in time and warn the vampiress of what is to come. Thus, altering the future."

"That is brilliant Joan!"

"I know."

****

1021 A.D.

I stabbed him repeatedly. I stabbed the king having lost all control of my senses. I was hurting. I hated seeing Nebuelah in his arms. I loathed even thinking of what he would do with her once in his bed. I punched at his throat and then grabbed Nebuelah pulling her into my arms and left his compound. The king's guards heard the noise and barged into his room. I managed to fight them off, running away with Nebuelah. I ran until I could run no more. I escaped into the forest still holding Nebuelah. She was so beautiful when she slept. I could hear rustling leaves close by. I watched the cool wind blow through her hair. Gently lifting Nebuelah's body off the ground, I carried her with me to a cave no one in my tribe had known about. I would often go there to be one with my thoughts. I was relieved and happy to be next to Nebuelah. I touched her thigh and stroked her legs, caressing its softness and smoothness, until I could not contain myself and went further up her thigh and began caressing the hair between her legs.

"What are you doing?"

"I want to make love to you Nebuelah!"

"What happened? Where am I?"

"I did it. I attacked the king so I could have you."

"You did what?"

"I wanted you all to myself."

"You fool! Your lovesickness for me will be the end of you. I was to handle the king myself. I would never have allowed him to bed me if I didn't want to. Why must you always take matters into your own hands?"

"I don't know what came over me, I just knew he couldn't have you."

"The jewel, you possess it still, do you not? I remember last when you stole it from me."

"Yes."

"Then that's it. Your desires were purely selfish when you stole it from me. It read your heart and saw that you would stop at nothing to have me and corrupted, as you were, it drove you mad and made you attack the king. You must hand over the jewel to me."

"Yes. Anything you desire my love". I searched for the jewel in my satchel. I could not find it anywhere on my person. "I seem to have lost it. I must have lost it when I was maddened with rage assaulting the king."

"No."

"Well, Nebuelah, I don't know what else to tell you."

"Had you not been in a mad rush to prove your worth to me, I would have told you that the power of the jewel has a mind of its own. Once the possessor fulfills his or her purpose, it encapsulates that power and moves onto another, more corrupt, more sinister being. I sense it may have moved onto an evil temptress, an undead being."

"How can that be?"

"Only a witch can wield its power. Once the jewel is no longer in the hands of a witch or warlock, it becomes, sentient of sorts, and feeds off of the corrupt. In so doing, it then craves only such energy and grows ever stronger, desiring only evil. At which point, it develops a mind of its own and seeks to find those who will destroy others for the mere sake of destruction. This is why only a witch, such as I, can possess it."

"I should have been more patient with you. I never seem to do anything right."

"Don't be so hard on yourself. Your heart was in the right place. I know how much you love me as I do you. But you needn't prove anything to me. Your heart is all I need."

"Nebuelah."

"Yes."

"Don't ever let me go."

"I promise I won't."

"Do you forgive me?"

"There is nothing to forgive."

"What shall we do about the king?"

"His army will go in search of the one who attacked him and they will have him hanged but I will try to hide you."

"I wish I had never…"

"Esuahway, you have done wrong. This is true but I can understand why you did it though I may not fully agree with your actions. You love me and you defied your beliefs, your kingdom, your people, all for a woman you know to be your one true flame. Love is blind and cruel but it's also caring, docile; very serene. You are such things to me. But please, Esuahway, don't ever feel you need to prove anything to me. You are already everything I could ever need."

In the following days, I learned that the king had miraculously survived his stab wounds. I was given a second chance to rule by his side and that chance was given in the form of killing a man in his stead. From the moment, I voiced my dissent and regret for having taken a life, I was exiled. And so began, my vampiric life.

****

I woke up with my heart pounding in my chest. I could scarcely breathe. Oh, I remember now, I don't breathe. I am, as you would say, in today's modern world, the living dead. But every once in a while, out of reflex, I mimic human behavior. Sometimes, I do it to remind myself of what I once was and sometimes I do it blend in with mortals. This time, I do it because I remember how compassionate Nebuelah truly is. It's all coming back to me now, why I want her, yearn for her and need her in my life. She understood me like no other. She was more than a lover; she was my friend. Why can't I let her go? Why must she always run through my mind? Even in my dreams, she is always there.

I could feel a throbbing sensation, suddenly, in my chest. I had never felt such an ache before. Sitting on the edge of my bed, I hunched over. I never feel pain so this was quite alarming for me. I stumbled to the bathroom and washed my face in the sink. I stared at myself in the mirror and saw the porcelain tint of my eyes, my straight but bushy eyebrows, my shoulder-length black hair, my aquiline nose, and the open expression of my eyes.

I yelled out in pain and fell over into the bathtub. The pain in my chest was intense to say the least and with nothing left to do, I lifted my shirt and could see emanating from my chest, the brightest light I had ever seen. I did the inevitable and cut myself open using my nails and pulled out of my chest what appeared to be a glowing stone of some kind. It was a jewel, similar to the one Nebuelah had taken into her core. In fact, it appeared to be its exact half. I was beyond surprised. This entire time, I had been its carrier. I was certain to have lost it, centuries ago. What was happening to me? I need you now Nebuelah. I don't understand anything anymore. I no longer know what to believe. Please Nebuelah. I know you can hear my cry. Where are you? What must I do to find you?

The jewel shone brightly in my hands. I could feel its power vibrating all around me. Looking down at my chest, the wound I had made had already healed. I was not about to put the precious token back into my chest. I would safeguard it until I could find Nebuelah.

I placed the treasured item under my pillow and went back to sleep. I would awake tomorrow night and decide then what to do with it. I am still in dismay that this entire time, a piece of Nebuelah's power, resided in me. I don't remember ever taking a piece of her jewel into me. I don't even remember if she willingly handed it to me. I am confused and lost now more than ever. Does this mean Nebuelah is still alive? I remember her walking away in the distance and disappearing before my eyes like a glimmer of light. Could she be near me? Does this mean I am meant to find her yet again? So many questions ran through my mind that I was beside myself but the daylight hours were still alive and my eyes were forced to close. I had succumbed to my slumber but tomorrow night, I would be renewed once more and my journey into self-discovery will have been revivified once more.

TWENTY-SEVEN

SENSATIONS, SENSATIONS

I repeatedly hit myself over the head. I was insane to have walked away. Esuahway must be perturbed and broken. I neglected that I had hidden half of the core, inside his body, centuries ago during one of our love-making sessions. He will, undoubtedly, awaken to this fact and then begin to seek me. He won't know what to do or be able to rationalize what is going on. I trust he has the sense to protect the jewel. I can sense that danger is imminent. I have to make my trek back to Canada and find Joan. Now, that I know *what* I am, I can feel she was never a friend of mine. She was no different than Ewan. She must have been searching for me for a long time and decided to befriend me, in my weakened state, thinking she could take my power from me. Now, that I am no longer my "mortal" self, I am fully aware of the danger she poses to both me and Esuahway. She has been trying to find my location through her dreamscapes. I am careful always to shield my face and my whereabouts so she cannot do me harm. But she ceases not with these pestering dreams of hers. She will stop at nothing to bring back Nephthys and claim her rightful place by her side as an unflinching and deadly henchwoman. The others in her clique: Marcus, Jack and Stella are merely pawns in her game. I am careful not to reveal any such findings to anyone. If they are pawns in her game, then so too shall they be pawns to me. I am more concerned, at the moment, for Esuahway. I have always kept information hidden from him and only told what I felt he needed to know, on my basis. I fear now he will have to fend for himself without the other half of my power. I must go to Canada and anticipate the worst. There is another battle ahead and I must be ready and willing to engage with formidable foes. I can hear Esuahway's cries out to me. I choose not to respond. I could very easily send my thoughts out to him but for his sake, I must not do so. Joan has already penetrated my mind once and to send out my response to Esuahway, she would easily detect his location. For now, he remains safe and so long as he protects the jewel, he won't have anything to fear. He is an incredible fighter in his own right.

KNOCK. KNOCK. KNOCK. So lost was I in my thoughts of Esuahway, that I was startled by the knock on my door. I have hidden myself in a dirt-filled motel, in Los Angeles. Unlike Esuahway, I choose to hide in the city amongst humans. He prefers the countryside. That was something the two of us could never agree on. I hid behind the door and briefly looked into the peephole. No one was there. I barricaded the door with the motel's dresser drawer and distanced myself about 10 inches from it. KNOCK. KNOCK. KNOCK. There it was again. I did not look into the peephole. I was hesitant, of course. KNOCK. KNOCK. KNOCK. Without warning, suddenly, the knocking became banging and in the blink of an eye, the door was unhinged and thrown in my direction. I narrowly escaped its throw by jumping into the air and grabbing hold of the ceiling.

Crawling upside down on the ceiling, I saw what appeared to be Marcus. It appears Joan has found my location and she sent one of her goons to fight me.

"Well, hey there, beautiful! Why don't I join you on the ceiling? I know what great power you possess or you can fight me as the man I am!"

"I would if you were a man," I laughed.

"Always the comedian Nebuelah."

"I was never one for laughing."

"You will be when I annihilate you."

"Give it your best shot," I retorted. He leapt up into the air and swung his arms at me, trying his darndest to tear me open. I kicked him so hard, he fell back and slammed into the wall, making a massive hole. The neighbor, next door, screamed in horror. I ran towards her and grabbed her by the throat but not so hard as to hurt her; I merely glamoured her. I told her she would remember nothing about the night's events. I then told her to promptly call the manager and report the damage done to her wall and that she was in the bathroom while the damage had occurred. She would then be placed into another room and sleep for the remainder of the night.

Marcus then speedily ran toward me and threw me over the balcony. I landed firmly on my feet and hissed at him. I ran toward my car and put the keys in the ignition and drove off. He followed me on his motorbike. I headed to the highway and drove off a beaten path nearing a forest's edge. I remembered an old shack not too far away from here and lured him there. Once inside the shack, I stood my ground and waited for him to appear. As soon as he blasted through the door, only seconds after I entered, he lunged at me and I leapt into the air, kicking him backwards with my foot. I ran into the basement and he followed me down the stairs.

"You have nowhere to go Nebuelah!"

"Really?!"

"Give me the jewel!"

"And why should I do that?"

"I think the better question to ask is why shouldn't you?"

I swiftly punched Marcus in the face and it knocked him backwards but only momentarily.

"Give me the jewel, bitch!"

"Such language. Honestly, Marcus I expected better from you," I said rolling my eyes. "Come closer sweetheart and I'll give it to ya!"

He rushed forward knocking me backwards when he head-bumped me, so I returned the gesture in kind by kicking him between the legs and punching him in the gut.

"This is nonsense! We could fight one another for hours on end and never get tired!" I shouted.

"Then let's end this – GIVE ME THE JEWEL NEBUELAH!"

"You'll have to behead me first."

"Is that an invitation?"

"I dare you," I stated.

"Then let's do this."

He started running toward me. I could see his movements but in slow motion; an ability no mere mortal can possess. He neglected to see the trap door, I had set up, weeks prior, fearing I would be attacked at some point. In a maddened rage, he pounced toward me. I grabbed hold of his grip on my neck and flipped him over and finally pushed him into the wooden floor. He fell through and landed straight onto the stakes I had planted into the ground. One stake went straight through his head. He was choking to death and bleeding from every orifice. I jumped down landing next to Marcus' head and spoke in his ear: "nice try and just so you know, I'll be dealing with Joan next. I won't let her get my core and I certainly won't let her reawaken Nephthys!" I tore his limbs one by one and wallowed in his screams. I tore his head off next and yes, sent it to Joan's location. I simply dropped his head off at her front door step in the sleazy motel she'd been hiding at in Nova Scotia.

TWENTY-EIGHT

GOLDEN YEARS

I don't quite remember the first time I saw her. It was as though she appeared to me as from a dream. It seemed as though she materialized before my eyes. I try to think back on how we first met and strangely enough, I can't seem to remember. She was ethereal, almost supernatural. The curves of her body, the glimmer in her eyes, the sheen of her hair. I felt as though I had been transported to another realm and she was the being that entered my realm from her own. I don't know when it happened but I felt a sensation in my stomach one morning, after she and I slept together. I never bothered to ask her what had caused the pain. I simply kept my remonstrations to myself. She was surreal to me. I often asked myself how I had even fallen in love with someone so inhuman. She was beyond anything I had ever seen. I wanted to know her better but there was always something...a veil of sorts that separated me from her and to penetrate it, would mean to decipher the essence of who and what she was. When I stared at her long enough, she didn't even appear female. I long, sometimes, to tell her my thoughts but I always feel as though I am offending her. I feel lost in her presence and confined to her realm whether I choose it or not. She is quite impressive in this feat; of always making me feel as though I am lesser than but somehow incompatible and even still incomplete when not in her vicinity. I even feel clouded when I'm with her. It's as though without her presence, I am lost to the winds.

There is always an aching in my heart when she lingers, when she's gone and when she's diminished in spirit. It's as though she has tethered herself to me and I have no logical reasoning or explanation for it. She is my world. She is my everything. And oftentimes, I find myself asking myself how it is I always feel that way. I do love her but sometimes I feel as though the love is so great that it overwhelms me; is beyond me and outside me. I have reasoned with myself that she and I simply glanced upon one another and knew it was love instantaneously and that that is how love is brought forth in this world but something lingers always in the back of my mind. It's an uneasiness that I can't explain. It doesn't bother me so much as it puzzles me. I just wish I knew the details of how Nebuelah and I truly consummated our relationship and the events that unfolded prior to our meeting. Most people can recall the details of the very moment they found their one true love. With myself, it was not so. Every attempt at recalling the founding of my union with Nebuelah is blurred. But then I look in her eyes and simply forget my troubles. It matters only that she is mine. Every time I look at her, there is a twinkling in her eye. It is something that I haven't seen in any other human. I mean to always ask her about her appearance but then I hang my head down and decide it best not to disturb her with my thoughts or questions. There is something about her that is out of this world. I wish she would let me in so I could see her for what she truly is.

Esuahway's Diary – October 21, 1946

Esuahway, you have pondered upon such things for so long. I should have let you entirely in when I had the chance.

It was wrong of me to shut you out. I made you love me and I never told you the full truth. If ever there was a time to reveal the truth, it is now. It is now or never.

TWENTY-NINE

JOAN'S REVENGE

"That bitch is full of it!" said Joan. "Who does she think she is?"

"She killed Marcus. It is apparent you will not retrieve the jewel," said Jack. "This woman will stop at nothing."

"She knows where we are! We should move NOW!"

"Maybe we shouldn't. Maybe we should lay low for now. Let her come to us and we could have a standoff."

"Hmm…yes, we could do that," replied Joan.

"Let her come to us. Let her begin the battle. The chase, after all, must come to an end."

"Perhaps, we could wait and set a trap for her here."

"True. This may catch her off guard. She may expect us to move but instead, let's let her come to us."

Hours had passed and finally, Stella joined Jack and Joan. They informed her of their plan to annihilate Nebuelah once and for all. They also told her that they wanted Nebuelah to bring the fight to them. Stella concurred that this was a good idea. They would, the three of them, set a trap for Nebuelah in the dingy motel room. Stella was more than happy to consign to this. Like Joan, she wanted to wield the power of the jewel but not to increase her vampire prowess tenfold but to seek vengeance upon those who killed her coven decades ago. The only bond that Stella, Jack and Joan had in common was that the jewel had immense power that all three wanted to yield in some way, shape or form. They were especially careful, this time, to plot Nebuelah's demise knowing she was anticipating them. She destroyed Marcus but together, she could not destroy the three of them united. Marcus, was foolhardy, he thought he would handle Nebuelah on his own given she possessed half the jewel. But he was, sadly, mistaken.

"Perhaps," thought Joan, "we could capture Esuahway and lure Nebuelah to us! She knows he possesses half the jewel. She must have bestowed it to him unbeknownst to him! That must be why he has survived as long as he has!"

"That's perfect Joan," answered Stella, "we could send a signal to Esuahway that we have his precious Nebuelah and he will come running to us! He will have to give his half of the jewel."

"We should make headway then," stated Jack, "we must go to Esuahway and lure Nebuelah and then we could finish them both off…at once!"

"Precisely," agreed Joan, "except we won't do this in the motel. Instead, we will take to the Acadian forest."

****

Esuahway was lying in bed, clutching still to the jewel in his fist, under the pillow. He allowed himself to rest as he never had; pondering the mystery of himself and his jewel. He dreamed of nothing. He wanted to forget, for just a moment, what had happened but a few seconds ago. Rest was all he needed and he would be rejuvenated. He would start the following day anew, knowing he would hunt and be refreshed once more with a victim's blood of his choosing. Just as he was about to fall fast asleep, he suddenly remembered his journal was lost to him. He had had it in the compound back in England and it was his treasured possession and now, suddenly he remembered he had left it behind. He wanted it. He needed it. His thoughts were encased in it. How foolish, he thought to himself, to have left behind the one document that detailed his account of Nebuelah. I will retrieve it when tomorrow I awake, he thought to himself.

The following evening, Esuahway awoke with a strange feeling he had not felt the night before. He was refreshed and eager to hunt but he could feel something lurking close within his vicinity. He was still slightly disturbed by discovering the jewel was within him and he wanted to write down his thoughts about Nebuelah. He must get back to his journal.

He paused for a moment because he heard a rustling noise outside his door. He ignored it for a moment and decided to exit the window of the bathroom and leap to the ground to make his escape. He could easily get to his car from the back of the motel. Again, he heard a shuffling noise outside his door and thankfully, given how large the window was in the bathroom, he decided to jump out the window. He landed firmly on his two feet and quickly ran from the back of the building to the side where he had parked his car. He could hear, in the distance, three individuals who had just crashed into his bedroom. He just barely made his escape and thankfully, with his life intact. He headed to his vehicle and started the ignition. He knew his life was in danger, though he could protect himself, he nonetheless decided to head to the Acadian forest, away from mortals so as not to harm them. If it's a fight, these contenders wanted, they would soon have it but away from prying mortal eyes.

Esuahway's foes were on his trail. They just barely caught him jumping out the window and followed suit by doing the same. They landed square on their feet and ran round the building to the front where their motorbikes were parked. They hopped on and were heavy on his trail. Esuahway put his foot to the pedal and headed straight for the highway and onto the path that led to the Acadian forest.

"Perfect!" shouted Joan, "he is headed straight the Acadian forest, right where we want him!"

"Let's get him!" shouted Jack.

The chase down the highway was inevitable. Esuahway zoomed past cars and Joan and her remaining minions followed closely by. More than an hour had passed till finally, Esuahway spotted the exiting lane heading toward the Acadian forest. He swerved in between cars, careful not to crash into anyone and tried to mislead the trio of bandits by driving onto a beaten path unseen to humans. He had made sure to learn of his territory prior to settling in Nova Scotia. He had learned of all the pathways and hidden trails for an event such as this. Continuing to drive on the beaten path, Esuahway was soon followed by the trio. One of the bikers was to the left of him, another to the right of him whilst the third was directly behind him. The one to the left of him tried thrashing at his window and ramming into the side of the car. Esuahway drove his car ramming into him, pushing him off the trail. The biker to the right hurled a tree trunk at his vehicle causing Esuahway to swerve off the path making his car turn over. He escaped out the front window of the vehicle and using his strength turned the car over before he was accosted by the third biker. He picked up the car and hurled it at Jack. Jack was crushed under the weight of the vehicle but in the blink of an eye, he threw it in the air and recovered quickly from this tumble. He ran, faster than the human eye could see, toward Esuahway, preparing to deliver a final blow, when he suddenly burst into flames. Esuahway stood, horrified, at the sight of Jack's demise. His fiery death was not his doing. He quickly turned his gaze to Stella and she was petrified still, just looking at Jack and not knowing what to do.

"Are you doing this Joan?" yelled Stella.

"No. Of course not!" answered Joan. "It must be you, Esuahway! You have the other half of the jewel. You are manipulating its power for your own use."

"I am doing no such thing!"

Stella, suddenly, began shaking violently. She was having uncontrollable seizures. "Help me," she said. "Please Esuahway, help me. HELP ME!" And just like that, she too, was set aflame. Her shrieks were unbearable. She was screaming until she could scream no more. The smoke had filled her lungs and within minutes, she was extinguished.

"Esuahway, STOP IT!" shouted Joan.

"I'm not doing anything."

"He's right. He isn't doing anything. I AM!"

I turned around to find Nebuelah was standing right behind me. I doubled over, falling to my knees, and began to cry out in pain.

"Stand Esuahway," said Nebuelah. "You are to stand before me."

"I can't," I replied. "I am in so much pain."

"It's the jewel. Do you have it with you still?" she asked.

"Yes. I secured it in my pocket."

"Your pocket? Really? And during the car chase, it never fell out once?"

"Well, I…"

"It doesn't matter. Give it to me."

I handed her the jewel and she took it with such force, I was momentarily taken aback by surprise. She gazed at it with such intensity, almost as if she were enthralled by it. And then without a moment's hesitation, she swallowed it whole and took it into her core. She has now fully regenerated into her true self. And what a sight she was to behold. Her hair was red and her flesh had transformed into translucent pale skin. You could see every vein in her body and she had fangs where there weren't any before. She turned round to stare at me with glowering eyes and tread slowly in my direction. Once in front of me, she picked me up by the neck and threw me a great distance in the air. I landed on my back, many feet away. She then ran, faster than I could see, towards Joan.

"Finally," shouted Joan, "a foe worth fighting!

Nebuelah merely growled. "Did you like my surprise gift à la Marcus?"

"You bitch. Let's end this!"

"As you wish."

The women ran towards each other and a battle ensued. The angriest fists of fury had been thrown, one after the other, in a never-ending battle of wits. I was merely watching in awe as the women were going at each other. I was shaken and yet enthralled all the same. I wanted to help Nebuelah but she threw me to the ground, obviously, not wanting my assistance.

The ache in my stomach had only gotten worse. I screamed for Nebuelah's help but she was otherwise engaged. "Please," I shouted. "Let me help you Nebuelah. I can fight alongside you."

"NO!" she shouted.

"Nebuelah, let me help. I care for you." I ignored her protestations and joined in the fight. I came at Joan from her side and struck at her with all my might, despite my pain. I kicked her and sent her flying in the air. Nebuelah leapt in the air and landed atop Joan, crushing her neck with her foot.

"You'll never have the jewel Joan, never shall I let you release the vampiress Nephthys. She is corrupt beyond your understanding."

"You only say that because you want all the power for yourself. Your worse than she ever was."

Nebuelah did not respond, she continued glaring at Joan.

"It was always about you Nebuelah, you and your selfish desires! You think you are so special. You didn't even tell your precious Esuahway the truth."

"What truth?" I asked. "What is she talking about Nebuelah?"

"She lies," Nebuelah replied. "Joan was never a friend to me. She was my handler. She was sent to watch my every move and prevent my re-awakening."

"Nebuelah, I don't understand. What is going on?" I pleaded.

"Yes, Nebuelah, tell him. Tell him how you used him this entire time."

"I don't know what you're talking about. I haven't used anyone."

"Haha! Nebuelah, you are the real liar around here. Move your damn foot off my throat. All of this, these wars, it's all your fault. And Esuahway, he was just a pawn in your game."

"Nebuelah, what does this woman speak of?" I pleaded once more.

"She won't tell you Esuahway because she's a coward. She is the most wicked, most deceitful, most self-centered witch that has ever existed! When he learns of the truth, I hope he rips your ugly face off!"

"Shut up Joan!"

"Nebuelah, please, tell me..." I begged of her.

"Don't listen to her.

"Oh no! Do listen to me. The jewel Esuahway, she made you *think* you wanted it for yourself. She made you take it by force. She wanted the king out of the way, those many centuries ago, because she wanted vengeance for the death of her people. She felt he took the throne by force and she needed someone to take the blame for his death and that sucker was you, Esuahway. You were never in love with this fiend. She just made you think that you were."

"Nebuelah, is this true?"

Nebuelah was dead silent. She looked at me with imploring eyes but said nothing.

"TELL HIM NEBUELAH. THE MAN HAS BEEN SUFFERING FOR CENTURIES BECAUSE OF YOU!"

"Enough! I am done playing games with you. I will end you right here and right now."

Nebuelah released Joan from her foot's grip and grabbed her by the neck, she tore her arms off and punched her in the gut. Nebuelah drank the flowing blood from her body and relished in it. She looked at Joan, directly in her eyes and whispered: "silly girl, you thought you could bring back the vampiress. Only the one who summoned her could bring her back and guess who that is? ME!"

Nebuelah squeezed her neck so tightly that her eyes bulged out of her head. She was losing consciousness and with the snap of her neck, her head slumped backwards and Nebuelah, using her Fire Gift, set her ablaze.

Nebuelah fell to the ground, bending over in the fetal position. The jewel inside her began to illuminate and her eyes started to bulge, her veins began protruding and her body was shaking uncontrollably.

"Nebuelah, what is happening to you?" I cried.

"Now that I've taken in the jewel, the complete jewel, my body cannot contain its power for very long. When I was a child, my mother, who was a witch herself, foresaw my future and knew I would have power even greater than her own. At birth, she fashioned the jewel from my tears, so she could raise me without fear of my power getting out of control. To take it back in, as I have now, is to no longer be subdued. I may die in this very moment."

"No. Nebuelah, don't say that. I love you."

"No. You don't love me. You just think you do. Once I became a young woman, all those centuries ago, and my village was attacked by the king – the very one you served – I wanted my revenge. I knew you were his steward and I needed to keep you close to me, so I could kill the king. So long, as you were in his vicinity, you would always protect him. Once I realized this, I decided I had to get you out of the way. I used the power of the jewel to make you fall in love with me. I would have my way with you. I controlled your thoughts and made you think that you wanted to prove your love for me by attacking the king who wanted me for a fourth wife. The only problem was my Mind Gift worked better than I had anticipated. I wasn't just controlling your thoughts; I *was* your thoughts. You stole the other half of the jewel, used its power to conquer the king and in so doing summoned the vampiress only you didn't really summon her. I did. I was fully aware that using the jewel would invite other beings into our world. For to use it, means to submit to one's lower self. The vampiress must have sensed this and entered our world. I made you fall in love with me, so you would not stand guard for the king. I willed you to annihilate him, because I sought vengeance for the death of my people. I made you yearn for the jewel."

"But why Nebuelah? Why?"

"Because…you were standing in my way of destroying the king."

The jewel's power was all-consuming. Nebuelah's stomach was rising and falling, her skin was stretching and her eyes were bulging worse than before, until I thought they would finally fall out of her head. She was holding her head in her hands because the pain she felt was unbearable.

"I think my head is going to explode!" declared Nebuelah.

"What is happening to you?"

"I wasn't meant to take the jewel back into my core. My body is collapsing onto itself. This is it Esuahway. My time has come, I will finally die. I will exist no more on this earth. Turn away from me. Do not watch me die."

"But I care for you."

"Esuahway, have you not been listening to me? I made you fall in love with me."

"No. I don't believe you. I don't believe that. I do love you. It all makes sense now. You said it yourself. The only real power is the manipulation of nature; to bend it to one's will. I must have been in love with you for you to manipulate me in the first place. There must have been some part of me that yearned for you, no? Nebuelah, don't leave me. I love you."

"Esuahway, please, stop saying that. I may have used you but you still have free will. When I perish, you shall forget about me and finally be free from me forevermore. You can find your way without me. I am the worst thing to have happened to you. And now, you have the freedom to explore the gift of your eternal life."

"I can't do it without you, my Nebuelah. Stay with me. Can you not will yourself to conquer the jewel's power? You are the very essence of Nature herself. Please, just try for me Nebuelah."

Nebuelah began convulsing in my arms. She screamed so loudly, I was deafened for a moment. Blood came out of every part of her body and she began choking on her own blood. Her body shriveled and before my eyes, she became a former shell of herself. Her beauty faded and in the twinkling of an eye, she was no more. She simply dissipated into nothingness. She vanished.

****

The jewel was all that was left behind but its luminescence was no more. It was a mere rock. I held it in my hand for several minutes just thinking it is now, the only thing, I have left of Nebuelah. I am beside myself knowing that the woman I loved was not the woman I thought she was. I was chasing a phantom the entire time. I couldn't believe that for centuries, I was nothing more than a plaything in her game. My feelings were never my own. I suppose now, all that is left to do, is re-learn how to trust in myself again and build a new identity for myself: one outside of Nebuelah and one that is solely and purely my own. It dawned on me then that I had never really truly known love. Or maybe, just maybe, love is being used by another. If there is one thing Nebuelah has taught me it's that love is dominion over another. Love is not without its faults and love is and always has been conditional. She was the one with the selfish desire all along and I was simply the means to an end.

THIRTY

STARTING OVER

It was hard at first trying to find a purpose to my newfound existence without Nebuelah. She was all I knew. I did, at times, miss her but I was not totally without direction either. During the final battle, I scanned her thoughts and went to Los Angeles, where last she had stayed. I went to the motel she had last resided in and scanned the room for any token of hers she may have left behind. The room was clean. Everything was taken out. Nebuelah was always very careful with her belongings and never would have left a trace of her existence in any given area. I took in the scent of the room and just stood there, for a moment, with my eyes closed, and let the essence of Nebuelah permeate my mind.

I left the room in about one hour's time, careful of course, to not let myself be seen by the motel manager or any other guests staying at the residence. I got into my car and drove to the airport. My next destination would be England. I wanted to go back to where this all began. England was where I had first seen Nebuelah after searching for her for so many years. A semblance of a mortal then, she was the key to my self-discovery. She was the reason I kept surviving for so many centuries.

It would be seven hours later; I'd arrived in England and I walked the cobblestone streets of London. I visited the museums and enjoyed the architecture of England's fine castles. I strolled past Buckingham Palace and I even took in a movie later in the evening. I travelled by taxi to Nebuelah's old apartment where she stayed. I stood against the lamppost and looked across the street and up into the room where I'd once stared at her. I was just staring and pondering how far I'd come since this all began. I stood for a good while across the street just reminiscing on everything that had transpired until suddenly, I saw a flash of movement in the bedroom. I waited a moment to see if it would appear again and after a few seconds, another flash of movement. I crossed the street and broke into the apartment from the back door. Always on guard, I snuck in through a window being careful not to make any noise. I heard a ruffling noise in the same bedroom Nebuelah once slept in and I hid behind a cabinet, in the living area, awaiting the moment when I could apprehend the stranger. Again, I heard the noises and I waited. At one point, there was dead silence in the room. I feared the creature must have suspected I entered the apartment. After all, if I was dealing with another creature such as I, he or she would have suspected another of its kind was near.

The noises resumed once more. A flash of movement escaped the room and headed toward the kitchen. I couldn't get a clear glimpse of it. Whatever it was, it was hard to see clearly or possibly it did not want to make itself known. In any case, I could not see it even with eyesight as powerful as mine and could not capture it as a result. It scurried about in the kitchen making plenty of noise in the process. It stopped abruptly when the phone rang and a voice message was left asking if Marianne was still interested in the job at Chrysalis Records. The creature picked up the phone during the recording of the message and abruptly said: "no, she is not interested. She has secured new employment elsewhere and apologizes for any time wasted."

The voice sounded familiar. It sounded like Nebuelah. But how could it be? Nebuelah perished the last time I saw her. Unless, this creature was mimicking her. Something had taken her form and was now impersonating her! What other explanation could there be?

I decided to continue waiting behind the cabinet. I made not a sound. I was unsure of what I was dealing with and waiting things out seemed like the best plan of action. After the creature hung up the phone, I heard it murmur. It made a faint sound similar to someone clearing their throat. It knocked over a vase and two lamps and then moved swiftly out of the window. I moved from behind the cabinet and chased it down but it had already made its way onto the street and headed past two blocks going westbound. Whatever it was, it was fast. I jumped out of the window and headed in the direction it fled in. I ran faster than the human eye could see and tried to pick up on its trail. It was difficult indeed for this creature was faster than anything I'd ever encountered. After running about five more blocks, I decided to give up the chase. It wasn't worth my time or energy. I decided I would head back to my hotel and enjoy the rest of the evening lounging in a restaurant.

I spent the rest of the night taking in the sounds and sights of London. I walked as I had always done, every night, in search of a fresh victim to satiate myself. I preferred to take people I did not know; sometimes the evildoer and sometimes not. The taste of blood was refreshing. It always brought with it a clarity of mind I could not find elsewhere. It was absolutely overwhelming the thrill of the hunt, the chase and finally the submission of my victim. I must admit I do enjoy the struggle my victims will put out; to feel life slipping so easily through my fingers and to encapsulate that entire moment in a luscious red gush down my throat. I revere life. I respect it. I never toy with my victims. Victims…hmmm…I thought to myself, I was once Nebuelah's victim? Would I, if I could start everything all over again, be her victim once more? Nebuelah, if you are out there, somewhere, in some shape or form, then hear my thoughts: did you ever really love me? Or was I one of several pawns in your game? How many have you seduced? How many have you misused? I believe you saw your mark when you saw me and I was all too eager to go along with your schemes! I may have fallen in love with a witch whose power knew absolutely no bounds but I was innocent and naïve and that is why you chose me. Tell me I am wrong Nebuelah. Tell me something I do not know.

THIRTY-ONE

RED HAIR

I went out to the Les Boutins nightclub. There were many dancers abound and like stars they were shimmering under the disco lights. I sat in the corner, in the dark, amongst two drinkers but never engaging with them. I contemplated what it was once like being human. I once ate bread, I'm sure of it and wine and beer. I remember the scent of fresh strawberries too. Do I long for such things? Not always. I have no regrets. I am what I am. My journey has brought me to where I am now. I cannot long for a past forlorn. And in the blink of an eye, there she was, like a celebrity out of a magazine, a woman dancing with long red hair. She swayed and bobbed up and down to the music like rising and falling waters. She was luminescent and vibrant, mystical and magical. She was eerie too. Her movements were almost inhuman. There was no one else dancing the way she did in the club. I gazed at her with eager eyes. I relished in her movements and was captivated by her every step. She was unlike anyone else; the way she danced. Every step she took was like watching someone walk on air. I was enthralled. I couldn't take my eyes off of her. I just stared and stared. When the music grew faster and louder, her steps changed with the rhythm and she rose higher and higher, it seemed, into the air, with every chord change. It was like watching a ritual right before my eyes. Suddenly, she stopped and stared directly at me. I averted my gaze and looked elsewhere. I turned round again and she was still staring at me. I didn't know what else to do so I waved at her. She looked at me sternly and then continued dancing. I sat still. I wanted to leave but I was suddenly approached by the woman and she asked me if I wanted to dance. "No, thank you." I replied.

I looked back to the dancefloor to find the woman with the long red hair no longer dancing. I scanned the entire club and could not find her. She was enchanting to say the least. She was beautiful. There was something about her that stirred my soul. She was like a faint memory that suddenly resurfaced from the back of my mind. She was like the fragrance of a lost perfume, from a lover, from a past forgone. She was exhilarating. And again, suddenly, she appeared from nowhere. She was on the dance floor yet again, enjoying herself. She pointed at me and beckoned me to dance with her. I reluctantly declined. She beckoned me yet again and again, I declined. I mouthed the words: "I don't dance." She mouthed back: "yes, you do!"

I was taken aback. I didn't know how to react. Again, she asked: "dance with me?" I didn't want to dance. She danced over to my table and pointed right at me. She grabbed hold of my hands and pulled me to the dance floor.

"The DJ is playing a slower song. Why don't you rock me back and forth?"

"I…don't…dance."

"Yes. You do. You just don't want to."

"Really?! How would you know so much about me?"

"Hmm...I don't know really; I'm just making assumptions."

"May I go back to sitting down? I don't really like to dance," I replied.

"Oh, don't be silly! I will guide you."

We began to sway back and forth to the music. She was holding me around my waist and looking up into my eyes. I would sometimes look away and then look back into her eyes. She never once looked away from me.

"So, tell me about yourself handsome."

"I don't know what to say."

"Hmmm...well, start with your name," she said.

"My name is Reagan."

"Reagan. Hah! You don't look like a Reagan."

"Then what do I look like?" I asked.

"Hmmm... you look more like an Osiris, or Akhmet or something ancient."

"Ancient? Why do you say that?"

"It's your eyes. You look young and old at the same time. You look like you've lived a thousand times. You look weary yet alive. I don't know how quite to explain it!"

She was absolutely beautiful. Standing so close to her, I was lost in her eyes. They were like pools of blue waters, rising and settling, clear yet shimmering.

"Are you alright?" she asked.

"Yes. I just got lost..."

"Lost?" she interrupted. "Why, you are right here with me, how can you be lost?"

"I meant...that...your eyes."

"My eyes?! Hahahaha," she stammered. "You are a delight, Reagan! Well, then don't get too lost in my eyes or I might just have to pull them out of my sockets!"

She laughed so heartily. I was drowning in the sound of her voice. It had such a power that I was overwhelmed momentarily in the sound and almost fell forward.

"Hang on there, Reagan, don't go falling on me," she smiled.

"What is your name, if you don't mind my asking?"

"My name is Lucinda."

"And what do you do for a living Lucinda?"

"I dance of course!" she laughed again.

"Do you?"

"No, silly. I work from home, I'm an interior designer."

"Do you like what you do for a living?" I implored.

"Yes. How are you enjoying dancing?" she asked.

"I guess with the right person, it's quite enjoyable."

"Am I the right person?"

"Yes. I suppose you are," I smiled.

"Oh wow! There it is! A smile on your face. You are very handsome Reagan. You should smile more often."

"I don't ever feel I have a reason to."

"Well, I hope that changes with me," she said jumping into my arms and tightening her legs around my waist. She told me to twirl her and I did. She was letting the music guide her and beckoning me to kiss her.

"I barely know you," I implored.

"Does that matter? Just kiss me."

"I don't know," I stammered.

"Don't be so shy Reagan or at least give me a kiss on the forehead."

I was apprehensive but I gave in to her demands and kissed her forehead.

"You are too kind Reagan!" she yelled.

"Yes. I suppose I am."

We continued to dance the entire night through until she became exhausted.

"Will you take me home Reagan?" she pleaded.

"Yes. You don't mind telling me where you live?"

"No. Not at all."

I walked her to my car as she was laughing hysterically in my arms. She was yawning, getting tired and nearly fell to the ground until I caught her.

"I live on 415 Alibaster Street. It's six blocks from here. Just make a left at every light and you should find my apartment."

I did as she asked and when we arrived at her apartment, she was fast asleep in my car. I carried her in my arms to the front steps. I found her keys in her handbag and then opened the door using only my right hand. I placed her gently in her bed and then closed the bedroom and left her there making sure to lock the door behind me.

"Always the gentleman," a woman from the shadows said.

"Who is there?" I asked. "Who is that?" I turned to the left and right of me and saw no one.

I thought I saw a shadow move swiftly past me. It was indiscernible. It was what I think I had seen back at

Nebuelah's old apartment; back when she was still "Marianne". Or was it? I wasn't certain but whatever it was, it was stalking me.

THIRTY-TWO

AN UNBRIDLED DILEMMA

I walked along the dark alley streets as always. After a night of successfully hunting and killing my prey, I disposed of the body and decided to head back to Nebuelah's apartment. The building had been closed but I entered through a back door, carefully unlocking the lock with my nail. I heard no rustling sounds this time around. I went through whatever belongings remained in Nebuelah's bedroom and those of her roommate and I found nothing unusual. Clothes, pins, books, a desk, a lamp, food packaging, etc. It was as any apartment with the typical décor you find in your average home. I went to the kitchen where I had killed Ewan and saw the faint outline of his remains where they once laid. It was surreal to see this place again knowing I was here but a few months ago. I rummaged through a living area cabinet and found my journal. The recollection of my poetry, my thoughts, my life's events, it was all there in my journal but how did it get here? I was beyond surprised. I never brought my journal on my travels with me. Every page was intact. There was one addition that was not there. It was a poem but not one I had written. The writing was obviously a woman's writing. But who could have written that? It read as follows:

Enticing and draining, it's the force of all life

It renders your heart still and seduces your fright
Drumming of the beat, aortic valves deplete
Intuitive and underlying, clusters muck and bleed
Wandering the forests, waters draining in the pond
I linger mesmerized and ponder forever long
Intensity breathes life, our hearts thump as one
For so long as I can remember, we are the same song
Life is but a dream they say, rivers running red
Beside me lay your head to rest, the warmth that is our bed
Blood is the lifeforce, the meaning of it all
I yearn for its cold embrace, I slumber in its fall
However, many takes it tries, however it may seem
I take essence in my palms, fall deeply into sleep
I cannot move past this realm, drink my soul to peak
Beyond the valve of holes, my blood it seeks to leak
Blood is all
Blood is life

I was curious now as to who wrote this. Her handwriting was very beautiful. Her cursive was very impressive. My mind raced with wonder at the thought of who it could be. I let myself re-read the poem thrice more. I lingered over every single word and let each syllable linger on my lips. I would just stare at the words and let them sink into my thoughts. I decided to keep re-reading the poem over and over and over again. Until, I could not read it anymore. I grabbed my journal and pocketed it in my jacket. I escaped through the back door and headed straight to my motel room.

I decided I would no longer frequent Nebuelah's old apartment. It was time I put that part of my life to rest.

****

Once I arrived back at my motel, knowing the sun would rise in about one hour, I undressed and decided to lay my body to rest on the bed. I kept my journal under my pillowcase and finally, closed my eyes and forced myself to sleep. I dreamed of nothingness. After so many centuries of living, what more is there left to dream of? I have seen many lands, met many kinds of peoples, seen the world's wonders and explored many oceans. I have assumed so many identities, and lived in many homes. I have re-fashioned myself into many identities that I've brought many of my desires to life. I am a walking epiphany; a reinvention of myself in perpetual motion. I see nothing and feel nothing when I dream. The astral part of my being has been lost to me for many years. I am the living dead, as humans would call it. I am and never will be truly alive.

Five hours later, I awoke to the sound of rustling outside my window. I thought I saw the same shadow figure I had seen when first I broke into Nebuelah's former apartment. It moved with such swiftness that even with my preternatural sight, I could not discern the creature. As old as I am, the sun does not bother me but I prefer not to stare outside during daylight hours all the same. I was dumbfounded at it all. I could feel the entity move swiftly outside my room. It knocked at the door and then knocked at the window. I wasn't so much perturbed as I was puzzled. After a few more minutes of this entity disturbing my sleep, it finally dissipated. I went back to my bed and shrugged off the day's event. I was not going to lose sleep over an entity that – twice now I have seen – but has yet to harm me. Perhaps something is trying to communicate with me. Perhaps I am merely exhausted and need to recollect myself; gather my mind and release some stress. But I could not fall asleep fast enough, I had to write in my journal. I grabbed my pen and decided to pen my thoughts on revisiting Nebuelah's apartment and my chance meeting with that mysterious woman at the Les Boutins nightclub. How strange that they both had red hair? I was going over the past day's events and then finally, something in me stirred. I was moved to re-read the poem penned by the mystery woman, once more. The line *"wandering in the forests, waters draining in the pond"* struck me. Why was this woman wandering the forests and looking for waters to drain in a pond? She then speaks of *"our hearts thumping as one"* when *"life is a dream as rivers run red".* It felt as though this poem was a message of some kind; not merely art. She must be a vampire of some kind. She speaks of blood being all and blood being the source of life! She follows this with *"for so long as I remember, we are the same song".* This message…I wonder if it's for me! I wonder if this woman, or entity, whatever it is, is communicating with me. This woman must have written down this poem, having once possessed my journal, prior to my final battle with Joan and her accomplices. Could it be that Nebuelah wrote this, at some point, without my knowing? She needs the *"essence in her palms to move past this realm."* I wonder, no, it cannot be. I wonder if the now powerless jewel is the key to all of this. Perhaps if I take the jewel to a river or flowing water of any kind, anywhere, that that is the key to bringing Nebuelah back to life? Is Nebuelah communicating with me from the dead? Or whatever realm she currently exists in? Is she trying to tell me something?

The following night, I read the poem or rather encoded message once more and went to the local convenience store to get a map of London. I searched for any nearby lakes or streams in the area. I thought if I could get myself to a body of water, I could revive the jewel's essence and this may bring Nebuelah back to life. No. Wait. How silly of me. I am thinking wishfully. She is no more. There are no poems or songs or enchantments to bring someone back from the dead. I am like a child. If Nebuelah were here, she would concur. But that was a quality in me she admired most of all, that I retained my inner child, something that very few grown-ups could do or frowned upon. This cannot be her communicating with me through writing. What am I thinking? What am I doing with myself? I thought I moved on with my life and put her to bed. I must be tethered to her still in some way. What would make me think Nebuelah is talking to me through poetry? I don't even recall what her handwriting looked like! I must be going insane. I went to my pillowcase and searched underneath it to retrieve the jewel but it wasn't there. Bewildered, I searched the entire room up and down, several times over and I did not find it. I opened the front door and surprisingly, it was at my doorstep. I do not understand, I thought to myself. I brought the jewel inside of the room with me. I would never leave something so precious outside. How could this be? Unless, it possesses some degree of power still, and can move of its own free will, I have no understanding of how the jewel – once inside my premises – came to be outside. I pondered for a moment and thought if the entity that was outside my room had anything to do with the jewel's movements. The more I think on it, the more I realize that the jewel may be the key to all of these mysterious events. I was eager to fathom further if my machinations were correct. I would take my map of London and mark X's on every body of water until my mind drifted to the River Thames. I would go there, at night, as it is the most famous bodies of water in England. With my supernatural speed and strength, I could reach the waters, hours after midnight, and perform the necessary ritual. I decided I would accomplish the task in a fortnight. I needed to recharge, and hunt a few nights more. As always, blood provides me with such clearness and peace that it is the closest remedy to restoring whatever remains of my soul; more than anything else in this world. My mind was set, I would test my hypothesis to see if the poem was an incantation to bring back Nebuelah in fourteen days' time.

****

After two weeks had passed, I set my sights to the Thames River. I would wait till approximately 2 am in the morning and join the river's edge. I would bring with me the torn page with the poem and the powerless jewel and see to it that I revivify the essence of Nebuelah. I placed the jewel by the water's edge, careful not to let the jewel float away and slit my palm to let the blood drop onto the jewel. I recited the poem and waited for something...anything to happen. I waited patiently once more and again, nothing happened. I re-read the poem and it suddenly dawned on me that I must *"lay my head to rest, the warmth that is our bed."* I laid flat on the ground, next to jewel and let myself hear my heart beat. I stared at the jewel with the power of intent and whispered *"Nebuelah"*. I did so many times over. I waited and waited and waited and received no response. No glimmer of light shone in the waters. I cupped the jewel in my fist and plunged the jewel deeper into the waters. I called out to Nebuelah and again, nothing happened. I closed my eyes and focused with such intensity that my mind thought of nothing else but her. I don't know how much longer I waited but again, nothing happened. So enraptured was I, in my desperation to bring back Nebuelah, that I accidentally let go of the jewel and it sunk to the very depths of the Thames River. I watched it sink to the bottom of the riverbed that I thought to dive in and retrieve it when I decided to simply let it go. Maybe, this is what is meant to happen. Maybe I am to let go of the jewel and this, finally, will sever the bonds that tether Nebuelah and I together. After so many centuries, this is the only true way to release her soul and let go of what's left of my own.

I returned that same night back to my motel room and enveloped myself in my ruminations. I would finally dream that night, of another world, where I would see as Nebuelah did. I was her. I knew what it felt like to be one with nature, to be as a witch, to be all-powerful. I was born to a great witch, with red hair, a woman so feared that the villagers bowed to her wherever she went. She was beautiful and yet she was feral even loathsome. She was a great leader to her people and commanded the forces of nature with such ease that she appeared to be one with nature. She birthed Nebuelah and trained her to be as powerful as she – a grand witch and guardian of time, space and nature itself. When Nebuelah, aged 16, was captured by my king, her people were destroyed. She was the last of her people and her mother was hung for simply being a witch. That was when Nebuelah changed and so powerful was her transformation that she awakened a demon dormant within her core. She knew how to contain its awesome power, but she chose not to. She would stealthily unravel my king's world and I was needed to accomplish the task. But I was feeling every moment, in my dream. I was as she was. I was entrenched in her emotions. I felt her wrath, I felt her anguish and I most definitely felt her pain. Without her mother, she was nothing. Without her people, she was lost. Her once proud, glorious race was no more and if she could not bring back the dead, she most certainly would satiate her vengeance. I cannot say I blame her. I most certainly would have done the same. I did not know my king was capable of such ferocity. I believed he was true and honorable. I was hypnotized at the beauty of Nebuelah's world. I understand now why they remained hidden from my people. Their kind were of unusual stock; they were humans yes but mythical. They had unlocked the secrets of ascension of our physical realm to dwell in the astral one at will. They had a great fortress surrounding their village that no mortal, fairy, or demon could pierce it. That was until the king, having disguised himself as one of their kind, using the power of a sorcerer of his own, had betrayed one of Nebuelah's people. He wanted complete destruction of her race so he could claim their lands for himself and in so doing, harvest the source of their great power. This dream, so vivid and lucid, shows me Nebuelah's origins and why her heart had become as hardened as it had. She was the *last* embodiment of truth, of righteousness, and hope of her people and to remain as such for always, she had to summon the vampiress to become immortal.

I awoke suddenly, in the middle of the day, having felt a stabbing pain in my gut. My vision of Nebuelah's life and history were rudely interrupted by this pain and so dumbstruck was I by this pain that I momentarily forgot who I was. I was Nebuelah, for a few moments. I could see her vividly emblazoned in my mind's eye and see as she saw. I was one with nature; one with source. I saw where last I had dropped the jewel in the Thames River and how far deep it had sunk. It was glowing. It was shaking violently and it was calling to me. I was not just one drop of water in the river, I was the entire river. I was the trees. I was the wind. I was the earth and the stars above. And with this new sight, I could feel Nebuelah was still alive somehow. So, elated was I that I could not even feel the weight of my body. It was as though I was air itself. The jewel, I had re-awakened it. I had resurrected its lifeforce. The power coursing through my veins was overwhelming. I was lifted off my bed by an unseen force and then just as quickly dropped down. I shook violently for a moment. My entire body felt like it was failing me and suddenly, I lost all consciousness. I could actually feel myself slipping away.

A month must have gone by or so it seemed, because the newspaper's date was November 21st. I can't recall when last I looked at a newspaper but the last time I saw the date, it was October 19th. I was no longer in the motel room but in an abandoned and neglected apartment on the outskirts of London. I don't remember moving places. Could it be that the dream had transported me to another location? Still holding the disheveled newspaper in my hand, I went over the last moments of my time in the motel. I was trying to remember what I could about my dream and most of it came in snippets but I could not quite piece it all together. I started to choke and grasped at my throat for a while. Without rhyme or reason, I suddenly coughed up a remnant of the poem. To say I was disturbed and shaken, would not have done any justice to my predicament. I could see a presence lurking outside the window. It was the same presence I had seen and felt back at Nebuelah's old apartment and the same one that jostled outside my motel door and window. This time, rather than being a shadow being, it had a solid corporeal form. It slid under the door and moved swiftly about in the room. It scattered from one end to the other. I barely glanced it. This being was faster than even I could see. It would knock me over a few times until finally, it just vanished into the air. Whatever this thing was, it could relocate at will and clearly, transport me to any location it desired. I finally collapsed onto the floor and let myself rest. When I felt satisfied that the creature would not return, I made my way to the door, wanting to leave the premises behind. Once outside, I was deeply moved. For I was not merely on the outskirts of London, I was back at my compound in England's countryside. I was back to where this all started.

THIRTY-THREE

CONFINES REDEFINED

My compound had been rebuilt and looked exactly as it had when I first purchased it. I am confused as I was certain Nebuelah and I had destroyed the building so as to detract our enemies. The entire facility – fully intact – in all its former glory was truly a sight to behold. I was at ease, for once. I was at peace. I was back on familiar territory and could rebuild back the life I once had. I walked the hallways of the mansion and entered every room. Everything from the curtains, furnishings, décor and lighting had all been the same. It was as though it had never been destroyed. I would rummage through the cabinet drawers and the closets followed by a quiet sit down in the library. I remember staring at Nebuelah, a then Marianne, devouring book after book. She was so serene as she read. I remember, as well, the unease I felt keeping her captive knowing who and what she really was. I never intended to imprison her as it is not in my nature to do such a horrific thing. It was painful to know I could not bring myself to explain things as I should have but in retrospect, I underestimated her inner strength. She would have rebuked me but later come to appreciate my efforts – or so I thought. This is all speculation. I continued to roam the building until I decided to move to the backyard. The gardens were lush and green. There were variegated flowers and bushes and all manner of creatures including butterflies, parakeets, and squirrels. I walked along the pathway and took in the sights and sounds. I laid my body down to rest on the cool grass. I let the wind blow through my hair and caress my face. I was carried away at the simplicity of it all. The night was upon me and soon the moon would rise in the sky. I waited patiently for nightfall and when it arrived, I looked up at the stars. I just sat in silence and took in the beauty of the night. I let myself be enveloped by it. I conceded to make the mansion my home once more. How and why, it has come into existence, I do not know. But I will make it my own. I will breathe life back into it and restore its glory forevermore. I have longed to be back home and somehow the universe has granted me this wish.

****

The waters were murky. I resurfaced after a month and had to will myself back to life. I could not even begin to describe the process except to say I was lost to everything I had ever known and had to gather all I could remember to bring back to life what I had known. The first thing that came to me was a mansion in England. I remembered a man had imprisoned me there and I fled for my life. Every time I tried to escape, he would capture me once more and imprison me. I am called to go back to this place and find the man who captured me. When I find this man, he will be the one to unlock the mysteries of my heart. I must concentrate on the power of my jewel to find his whereabouts. This jewel that is inside me is the key to it all. It's covered in his blood. I know I am on the right path; I can sense his presence, his languor. I can see him vividly in my mind, looking up at the stars. I remained still sitting by the edge of the waters. It was dark out and not a soul was close by. After a moment's rest, I would begin my walk, always remaining unseen. Like a flash of lightning, I could see now everything that had passed: my imprisonment by Reagan, the battle with the dogmen, the battle with Nephthys, my falling to my death off of a cliff, my defeat of Joan and her minions and my decay into nothingness once I took the power of the sacred jewel into me. What was a lifetime of events was reduced to a mere blip in time. It was surreal yet very real. I would begin my trek having had a moment's rest and then make my way to him.

THIRTY-FOUR

REALITIES COLLIDE

I heard a rustling at the library window. I turned to look and saw nothing. I continued reading my book and shortly thereafter, I ventured into the bedroom where I had kept Nebuelah and stood by the doorway. I imagined her presence lingering still on the bed sheets. I was moved to grab hold of her and take her in my arms but she existed only in my imagination. I would take only air into my arms and imagine the scent of her hair. I never did get to hold her the way I should. I was always very weary to touch her. I never knew when or how to approach her. She used to intimidate me. She still does. I was hopeful still that in time everything would make sense. How my mansion came to be? How I found myself back in the home where this all started? I decided to spend the day slumbering. I would dream, perhaps, once more like I used to and receive an abundance of clarity the following night. This time, I laid on Nebuelah's bed. I shut my eyes and let the sheets cradle my body. Everything that weighed my heart down, I let go. I would allow the sun's light to seep in through the curtains but only so much. I was immune to its effects but I preferred still, out of habit, to hide from it. Tomorrow, will bring new insights and new yearnings. Tomorrow, will bring change. I will create for myself a new identity, in this new age. I will go out and see the world for all of its glorious modern forms. For now, the night shall reinvigorate me. Slumber is my lover and only friend; the last place of refuge for a weary soul such as mine.

****

Once I found the mansion, I stepped inside stealthily, and I did so without so much as a shuffle. I climbed up the back walls and using my nail, cut a small circle into the glass window, breaking it and finally allowing myself in by unlocking it. I remember the compound very well. I walked quietly; always being careful not to make a sound. I remembered when I was first taken in by Esuahway, I was placed on the second floor. I looked about me, in every direction. I glanced inside every room. Once I reached the second floor, I knew my room was on the right-hand side and the third door down. I levitated off the ground about an inch and made my way down the hallway. This was an ability I had always possessed but never felt necessary to use. Because I did not want to make a sound, fearing what may or may not be in this residence, I chose to lift off the ground so as to catch an impending foe off guard. I moved about as a ghost, and when finally, I reached the third room, I descended with both feet firmly on the ground and found a chaise at the far-right corner. I made my way to it and sat on the chair. I looked out of the window and kept to myself. I manifested this residence. I manifested my resurrection. And I did so because Esuahway held onto the jewel. He was clever enough to recite the poem and decipher its message. I knew he could do it. If there's one thing my love could do, it is decipher clues. He never gave himself the credit he deserved but he was always very intelligent. And although I never told him as such, I did prize his mind. He was handsome of course and there wasn't an inch of his body I did not like but his soul was most precious to me. He possessed an inner beauty and a child-like purity that you seldom see in people. And despite his being a vampire, the true essence of his core, never faded. He was still a gentle creature and always so resilient. My astral form had seen him carry home the woman he danced with at the club. I had not yet fully regenerated but I was always near him. I had just enough strength to gather his journal and place it in the motel. It took all my strength to do so but the fact that he was still tethered to me gave me just the right amount of energy to accomplish the deed.

After the destruction of his mansion, I willed it back to its rightful place, brick by brick, only this time, unbeknownst to him, it is protected by a forcefield that is self-sustaining. No creature, werewolf or demon, fairy or vampire, can penetrate its force. So much was taken from him as a result of my actions, I thought it fair to give back the one thing that brought him some semblance of peace.

Had I not wanted vengeance for the king's destruction of my people, Esuahway never would have suffered an eternity as the living dead. He did not choose this fate – I did. I made the choice for him and this was unfair of me. I only hope that when he awakens, he will find it in his heart to forgive me. I do care for him, very deeply. I love the purity of his heart. From the moment, I saw him, all those centuries ago, I saw my twin in both body and soul. I saw the person I was to become.

I saw my ever growing potential and I saw my destiny unfold. He and I were meant to be together; now and forever. Did I manipulate the love I had for him to my advantage? Yes. I do not deny that I did this but I cannot manipulate that which was never there. He loved me all the more and that was something that was always in his heart.

I may have manipulated it but I never once forced his hand into mine. I sat in silence and waited patiently for the beauty of the night's arrival. I stood up for a brief moment and stared at my reflection in the mirror. I don't remember when last I looked at myself in a mirror. I looked the same and yet was different. My eyes were green like the jewel. My body appeared to be the same. My hair was a shimmering mix of red and black strands. Aside from that, I appeared the same as I always have.

My powers had grown tenfold since last I fought in the great battle with Esuahway. I have not only regenerated into the woman I once was, I gathered more power from the other realm, than I ever had before. I stood, for a few more minutes, just gazing at myself and then moved back to the chair in the corner of the room. I simply looked about the room and felt the smoothness of the satin curtains. I examined every inch of the room, letting my eyes settle on the details of the wallpaper, and the borders of picture frames. I felt the softness of the velvet chair beneath my legs. I rested in the comfort that Esuahway brought me back just as I knew he would, proving he is a great sorcerer – he just doesn't know it yet! Yes, that's right my love, you are a sorcerer and a vampire too. You have passed the test. You are worthy of being at my side and together we shall create a world of our own. With a love like ours, a bond unbreakable and pure, we will conquer all. Our powers combined will know absolutely no bounds for we are the creators of our destiny. You and I, Esuahway, always.

THIRTY-FIVE

AT LAST

I felt renewed, alive and blissful. A beautiful day's rest can do so much for one such as I. A vampire's powers are reinvigorated and replenished. I sat up on the edge of the bed, pondering the mystery of myself and what venture next, I would take on. I held my head in my hands and let myself simply be. I removed my jacket and my shoes. I was so exhausted, the night before, that I had forgotten to take them off. I stood up and massaged the back of my neck. I ran my fingers through my hair. I walked to the mirror and rubbed my face in my hands. I stood for a moment looking at my reflection and never once really taking in the vampiric changes that had altered my body. My eyes were glass-like, or as Nebuelah once perceived, like polished tin. When she wasn't fully herself, she must have been petrified to see such a sight! I went to the bathroom and washed my face once over. I returned back to the bedroom and sat once more on the edge of the bed. I took a few deep breaths, out of habit, and then closed my eyes. I concentrated on feeling the blood flow through my veins. I focused my energy on feeling the very essence of my vampiric nature with all my might. I lingered for a moment just letting go of everything that had happened and fortified myself with the thought that I would venture out, today, with a newfound look on life. My new identity awaits me and so too, does my new destiny. I took one more deep breath and stood up. I went to the room across the hall and searching through the cabinet, found a pair of denim jeans and a cashmere sweater. After a change of attire, I went back into Nebuelah's room and walked to the window. I opened the curtains and looked out the window and imagined the night beckoning me. There is nothing more mesmerizing than the night's stars. I enjoyed the view from the bedroom, for one last second, and then headed for the door. As I was about to exit my residence, I suddenly forgot my journal. I would often sit in cafes, and write in my journal whilst observing the people walking by. I would often write about recollections of past events, and sometimes my observations on human behavior but mostly, I wrote poetry.

I headed back up the stairs to the second floor and entered Nebuelah's room. I went through every drawer and cabinet and even checked under the bed but could not find my journal. I knew it had travelled with me when I was transported back to this place but now, it seems to have been misplaced. I searched once more through every crook and crevice and still, I could not find it. I surveyed the entire premise and then saw a chair in the far-right corner of the room. I walked over to it thinking the book may have been left on the seat. As I bent over, looking the chair up and down, I could see a faint outline of a person. It caught me by surprise but I was not disturbed. How could someone have been in the room without my noticing them?

"Because, my love, that someone is Nebuelah."

Esuahway – pronounced S-YOU-AH-WAY
One who continually seeks to find his path or way in life.

Nephthys – pronounced NEFF-THIS
A goddess who symbolizes the death experience.

Nebuelah – pronounced NEBB-YOU-LAH
A visible bright or dark mass against a luminous matter in the sky.

About the Author

Born and raised in Montreal, Ariell first began writing at the age of four. She first wrote poetry and song lyrics and later, during her academic career, wrote formal essays and short stories. She won the Commonwealth Award for her original poem "The Diligent Snowman" in 1994, the Humber Essay Writing Award in 2005, and was Rights & Permissions Director and Sales Manager for William Schaill's historical novel "The Admiral on Trial" in 2010. She has been an active member of the Golden Key International Honor Society since 2009. Ariell holds bachelor's degrees in professional writing, English and Nursing. She currently resides in southern Ontario, Canada.

About the Cover Illustrator

Olha Melnyk is a talented and vibrant children's illustrator and character designer from Ukraine. She always features diverse characters in her projects and continually produces exciting and vivacious work on Fiverr.

www.ingramcontent.com/pod-product-compliance
Lightning Source LLC
Chambersburg PA
CBHW020306030826
48979CB00029B/2193/J

* 9 7 8 1 7 3 8 7 6 8 8 2 0 *